Miserable Adventure Stories

Alex Bernstein

Prom on Mars
New Jersey

Some of the stories here have previously appeared in print or online at *New Pop Lit*, *The Big Jewel*, *Blue Skirt Productions*, *HeadStuff*, *Defenestrationism*, *The Zodiac Review*, *Saturday Night Reader*, and *Gi60*. Please rush right now to each of these sites and check out great works by much less depressing authors.

ISBN 978-0-9913135-7-0 (ebook)
ISBN 978-0-9913135-6-3 (print)

First print edition, December 2017

Published by Prom on Mars.
Please visit us at www.promonmars.com.

For Mom

Contents

The Rottweiler

It was a cold, brittle day in late December when I came to the apartments of 442D Butcher Street, London, and met my cousin, the illustrious Sir Roderick Rottswilde for the first time. But Sir Roderick was known by another more famous name. He was familiar to all Londoners as not-quite-the-World's-Greatest-Detective, and second-only-to-that-august-personage-himself-Mr. Sherlock Holmes. My elder cousin was, in fact, *The Rottweiler*.

And now, Sir Roderick – The Rottweiler – had done the impossible. He'd recovered the Crown Jewels themselves and waylaid the brigands who'd stolen them. Now, amidst a sea of reporters, he was turning both over to the highest-ranking officers of Scotland Yard.

"Yes, yes, yes! Gather round! Come on then," said Sir Roderick. "Squeeze in! There's room for everyone! Woolsy! Do keep the doors closed – that wind is awful!"

"Sir Roderick! Sir Roderick! Rotty!" The press couldn't contain themselves. Sir Roderick looked pleased as punch.

"Ladies and gentlemen of the press, beloved officers of Scotland Yard, friends and associates – I will now present to you three of the most heinous blackguards known throughout London. Indeed, these louts had the audacity to pilfer from the Towers of London! And they would surely be halfway to South America by now, if not for the superior deductive skills of...The Rottweiler!"

He bowed, graciously, and the room erupted in *huzzahs* – mine, perhaps, loudest of all.

"But how?! *How?!*" shouted one reporter.

"If I told you that, my friend, you certainly wouldn't pay five pence a copy to read Colonel Woolsy's account of it in *The Straggler* this Sunday! But you can be certain that – for your well-earned coin – therein lies a tale with all the intrigue, spills, chills, and derring-do that you've all grown so accustomed to. Isn't that right, Colonel Woolsy?"

Colonel Woolsy, distracted by nothing in particular, had missed his cue.

"*Isn't that right, Colonel Woolsy?*" Sir Roderick said, gently slapping him in the back of the head.

"Yes, yes!" harrumphed Colonel Woolsy. "Read all about it! Derring-do!"

"Show us the thieves!" yelled one reporter.

"Ah, yes, the thieves! Bring them out, Mrs. Hoover!"

Mrs. Hoover, Sir Roderick's spindly landlady, marched out three of the nastiest, most loathsome, non-clean-shaven hoodlums I'd ever seen – all shackled to one another at the hands and feet.

"First," said Sir Roderick, "we have Black Jack Lymon – a ruffian known for his keen interest in bludgeoning London bobbies with his favorite blunt instrument."

"*In-deed!*" roared Black Jack, proudly, his ebon mane bristling. The police in the room gave a collective shudder.

"Don't get too close," said Sir Roderick. "He hasn't eaten in five minutes. Next, we have Aleutious 'Squinty' Leicester. Squinty's criminal mind works so quickly that having both eyes open produces too much information for his diabolical mind to bear; thus...*the squint!*"

"I see ya! I see the whole lot of ya!" said Squinty, hunched over in that way that nefarious felons do.

"Thank you, Squinty. And finally, perhaps the most insidious of the trio, Alphonse LaMurge, aka 'The Detonator' aka 'TNTommy' aka 'That Bomb-Making Guy' aka 'Say, Alfie, what's the lit stick you're holding there?' aka – well, you get the idea."

"BOOM!" shouted LaMurge – causing the entire room to crouch quickly and cover their heads. He then erupted with a maniacal "*AH HA HA HA HA HA HA HA HA!*"

"What's a bomb-maker without a sense of humor?" said The Rottweiler. "And now, it's my pleasure to turn these fiends over to London's finest. And to accept from them my terribly insignificant finder's fee. Thank you."

The head constable handed Sir Roderick a fairly large sack.

"And now," said Sir Roderick. "I bid you all a 'Good Afternoon,' and a very happy holiday."

"Sir Roderick! Sir Roderick!" one reporter yelled. "What about Holmes?!"

"Yes!" said another. "He's been missing for weeks! Will you aid in the search for him?!"

"Look," said The Rottweiler, seeming extremely peeved. "Holmes – that great and brilliant detective – is probably doing what he does every year at this time – lounging in some far east opium den! And if not – well, he's such a super-genius, I'm sure he can find his own way home. Thank you! Thank you! Pick up *The Straggler!* This Sunday! Thank you!"

And with that, Mrs. Hoover ushered all reporters, police and brigands to the door, until only Sir Roderick, Woolsy, Lieutenant Grimsby and I remained.

"A-hem," said Lieutenant Grimsby.

"Oh good," said Sir Roderick. "Someone with no sense of when to leave."

"Have an urchin for you, Guvnor," said Grimsby.

"Sorry, I'm off fish today," said Sir Roderick.

"Not fish kind, Guvnor – *boy* kind."

"Ah. Orphan tours are Thursdays," said Sir Roderick. "Don't forget to buy tickets. Thank you!"

"'E's not an orphan, Guvnor. 'E's got a blood relative. 'e does."

"Wonderful," said Sir Roderick, sifting through his mail. "I suggest you drop him off with that wretch, then."

"Very good, Guvnor," said Grimsby, and with that he disappeared.

Sir Roderick glanced over at me, confused.

"Woolsy," he said. "Why's that boy still here?"

"I think," said Woolsy, harrumphing again, "*you're* the wretch."

"Oh no," said Sir Roderick, rushing to the window, and calling down to the street. "No! No! You! Come back here!"

"I'd say we have a new houseguest, Rotty!" laughed Woolsy.

"We most certainly do not," said Sir Roderick. "Don't get cozy, boy. You're not staying."

"I have a note, sir," I said, fishing a worn, rumpled paper out of my pocket.

"I don't want to read any notes! I want no more information than I've already –"

"Give it here, boy," said Woolsy. "I'll take a look."

Sir Roderick glared at me.

"Well, what's your name, then?"

"A," I said.

"A? Just 'A'?"

"A, sir. It's the only name I've ever known, sir. It was embroidered…on this." And I handed him my most prized possession, a soiled, worn-through rag.

"What's this?"

"My swaddling diaper."

Sir Roderick dropped it in disgust – which was how most people reacted to it.

"You only had one?"

"That I know of, sir, yes."

"And you've been carting it around for all these years…because…?"

"It's the only connection I've got to family, sir. You see the monogram?"

Looking as close as he could bear to, Sir Roderick saw the name.

"A. Dodger. Dodger? Oh…Oh no…"

"Relatives, Rotty?" asked Woolsy, still trying to decipher the note with a spyglass.

"Distant. Distant, distant, distant. Extremely. A bad lot."

"Well…according to this," said Woolsy, "the boy – and his closest living relative – stand to gain let's see –"

"14 million –" I added.

"– pounds upon the boy's 16th birthday. Such sum to be held till then by the Bank of London."

"14?" said Sir Roderick, studying me. "And how old are you, boy?"

"Almost 13, sir."

"That's another three years, thereabouts," said Woolsy.

"Oh, please let me stay, sir! I've read all your exploits! I know I could help The Rottweiler in his work."

"*14 million!*" said Woolsy.

"Somehow, I've a feeling it won't be worth the money. Alright, boy! We'll have a *brief* trial period. But one step out of line, and you're out."

"Thank you, sir."

"Where'd you grow up, anyway?"

"In a wayward boys' home, sir. Living conditions were miserable, filthy and horrible."

"Oh good. Then you'll feel right at home in our stables."

"Thank you, sir! Your kindness is immeasurable."

"It is, isn't it? Tell me, boy. What do you know about dogs?"

"Dogs, sir? What kind?"

"Rottweilers, of course."

Life with Sir Roderick was hard, but pleasant. I was responsible for polishing his boots, clothes, carriage, all the floors of his apartments, mucking out the stables where I slept and ate, and of course tending to the dogs: two monstrous, black, mentally deficient Rottweilers that salivated buckets and buckets of glop.

But I longed to spend more time with Sir Roderick, himself. I had followed his adventures in *The Straggler* for years – when I could nick a copy – and I knew deep down that he was even better than Holmes, no matter what the papers said. So, you can imagine my delight when the Bank of London genealogist determined that he and I might actually be blood relations. On that day my life changed forever. I had lived twelve years in filth and squalor, but now, not only might I actually get to live in a real house, with a real family – but with the world's greatest detective.

"Slop out that manure yet, boy?" called the stable manager.

"Doing it now, sir!"

Yes, life was grand.

Once, when I was in the middle of polishing the 12,000 floor tiles in the Great Hall, I overheard Sir Roderick and Woolsy discussing the most recent report concerning Holmes.

"Still missing," said Woolsy. "Been weeks now. *The Observer* suggests a kidnapping."

"Good," said Sir Roderick, putting a golf ball into a priceless Greek urn. "We'll be rid of the git once and for all."

It was too much. I couldn't control myself.

"Sir Roderick! You've got to rescue him! You've got to!"

"Who's this again?" asked Sir Roderick.

"Dodger," said Woolsy.

"Oh yes. Is he 16 yet?"

"Mm…Two years, seven months."

"Sir," I implored, "you've got to help Holmes! He could be in terrible danger! If the police can't find him –"

"Shouldn't you be de-licing the hounds or something?"

"Done, sir."

"And the horses?"

"Before the hounds, sir."

"And Woolsy…?"

"Yesterday, sir."

"Well, do the hounds again. You'd be surprised how quickly they breed."

"The hounds, sir?"

"The lice."

A few nights later, I awoke from my sleep to a distant clattering – as if someone – or someones – had broken into the house. And though I was forbidden to visit the inner halls at night, I snuck inside anyway and cautiously searched room to room. As I neared the expansive fireplace in the den, the sound grew louder. Looking closer, I brushed against the flue lever, dislodging it. Just then, the entire fireplace gave way, opening to a darkened set of stairs leading down. Nervously, I descended and found myself in a long, dimly lit hallway. The clattering grew louder, but now there were voices – shouting – not one, but many. I soon came to a large metal doorway. I pressed against it – just enough to creak it open – when suddenly it gave way and I fell through with a thud.

Inside was a massive, brightly lit hall – something like a counting room crossed with a saloon, and mobbed with more lay-abouts, hoodlums and madmen than you'd think London had to offer. The mood was bacchanalian. Men and women danced, carousing, and shouting to one another. My presence was hardly noticed at all. And as my eyes adjusted, I realized that – in the center of the room – stood Sir Roderick and Woolsy. My instinct was to rescue them.

"Sir Roderick! Don't worry! I'll get the police!"

With that, a hush fell across the hall, and hundreds of angry eyes turned towards me. I ran to the door, but it slammed shut before I could exit. Then the mob moved on me.

"Get your filthy hands off of me!" I shouted.

Sir Roderick and Woolsy pushed their way through to me, yet regarding my situation with little more than curiosity.

"Well, he's in on it, now," said Woolsy.

"I suppose," concurred Sir Roderick.

"What?! What's going on?!" I said. "Who are these thugs!?"

"These 'thugs'," laughed Sir Roderick, "are *my team*. May I present to you, *the Butcher Street Semi-Irregulars!*"

The entire mob laughed horrifically. And then out stepped Lymon, Leicester, and LaMurge – the three criminals The Rottweiler had sent to jail scant weeks ago. They, too, laughed and pointed at me. It was too much to comprehend, and at that moment I succumbed to these horrors and lost all consciousness.

I awoke, hours later, in Sir Roderick's study. Only he and Colonel Woolsy were there. And I prayed it had all been a bad dream.

"Drink this," said Sir Roderick handing me a glass.

"What is it?" I asked.

"Brandy," he said. "It'll make you feel better."

I sipped. It was foul, nasty stuff.

"It makes me feel worse."

"Well then, keep drinking." He strode about the room. "The way I see it – we have two choices. We bring you in on our little scheme –"

"Or?"

"We kill you," harrumphed Woolsy.

I choked and spat out the brandy.

"*Will you please stop harrumphing?!*" snorted Sir Roderick to Woolsy. "God, that's annoying!"

"Sorry," said Colonel Woolsy, embarrassed and trying his best not to harrumph.

"Kill me!?" I said

"On the plus side –" started Sir Roderick, "if we kill you – we wouldn't have to put up with all your fuss and noise all the time. On the negative side...mm...Woolsy, what was the negative side, again?"

"*The mess.*"

"Right..."

"And the money," he added.

"I won't make noise," I cried. "No fuss!"

"Alright, then. Here it is: I imagine – like most modern-day children – you believe with all of your precious little heart that The Rottweiler is some brave, good, insanely brilliant detective? Am I right?"

"Yes, sir! Of course!"

"Well, he's not, boy. The fact is – he – I – *I'm a thief.*"

And Woolsy nodded, in affirmation.

"A what?"

"A thief. A very good – no – an extremely *brilliant* thief! Honestly, I'm likely the best all-round criminal genius London's ever seen."

"Except for M," said Woolsy.

"Who's probably a *myth*," said Sir Roderick.

"But – you're not a thief!" I said. "You're a hero!"

"I play the hero. But it's a fiction, boy. The men and women you encountered earlier – they and I have an extremely accommodating arrangement. We commit crimes – and then I –"

"The Rottweiler!" corrected Woolsy.

"Solves them."

I was stunned. I couldn't believe what I was hearing.

"But the jewels," I said. "You recovered the jewels!"

"Did I? Well, let's see – first my men – Lymon, Leicester, and LaMurge – stole the jewels – one of my finer plots, recently – and brought them to me here – where I could announce that I'd recovered them. I then turned a fake set of the jewels over to Scotland Yard, along with the men who stole them. I collect the recovery fee. Woolsy pretties the whole thing up in *The Straggler* and The Rottweiler's reputation as a highly sought-after detective grows."

"*That's horrible!*"

"Yes, well – this might be a very good time to choose your words judiciously, don't you think?"

"And those three men? They just rot in jail?"

"After we turn them over to the police, we – ah – typically arrange for their –"

"Release –" offered Woolsy.

"Yes, well, I can't just go abandoning my men, can I? Kill the whole operation, really."

"But the police – someone will eventually realize the jewels are false!"

"Of course. And if I know Scotland Yard they'll beg me to help find them all over again!"

Rage filled me.

"You're despicable!" I said.

"It's true."

"You're a thief and a cheat and a liar!"

"And a scoundrel! Don't forget scoundrel..." offered Woolsy.

He and Sir Roderick seemed quite pleased with themselves, which made me even angrier.

"I don't believe this! Millions of people read about you! They believe in you!"

"And I truly hope," said Sir Roderick, "that they'll continue to do so. Magazine royalties are what –?"

"Eight percent of total net revenues," offered Woolsy.

"I understand," said Sir Roderick, almost tenderly, "that people need stories of adventure, of good men righting wrongs – and that's exactly what we give them. And quite successfully!"

"But it's all lies! You're not a real hero!"

"My boy – if there's anything I've learned in life, it's this: *there are no real heroes.*"

"There are!" I said. "Sherlock Holmes!"

And Sir Roderick's eyes blistered with a rage I had not yet seen. He looked around for a thick gold bell on his desktop and rang it fiercely. Immediately, two thugs entered the room.

"Lock him up, until we can figure out what to do with him!"

"You don't have to do this!" I shouted. "I believed in you! I still do!"

And so, for the next few days I was locked in the stables and forgotten. I was miserable. Of course, I had known hardship in my life. What bothered me was that I had truly believed in the myth of The Rottweiler – and I was so terribly disappointed. I packed my things. I had spent a good part of my life running. I could certainly run again. And yet…maybe there was something more I could do.

"Sir Roderick! Sir Roderick!"

"What?! What?!" Sir Roderick awoke in bed, alarmed. I was there, across from him, crouching on his reading chair. "How did you –?"

He reached for his bell, but I showed I had it in my hand.

"Give me that!"

"I've decided," I said. "You're going to rescue Sherlock Holmes!"

"Piss off," he said, sinking his head back into the pillow. I leapt onto his bed and jumped up and down on it.

"Come on," I said. "It's the perfect thing!"

"For who? You?!"

"For everybody! For you –"

"Me?"

"Then you'll be a real hero?! You really will be everything you pretend to be!"

"Boy!" He said, sitting up and holding me still. "I *like* what I pretend to be! I enjoy it! I do it well! And I make a frightening amount of money doing it *exactly* the way I do it. No one in this house is looking to change a bloody thing!"

"I don't believe that! And I don't believe you! Not for a second!"

"Go back to your room!"

"I won't," I said. "You know what I think?"

"No – but I've got a horrible feeling –"

"I think you started out as a real hero – and when it got to be hard work – you took the easy way out – *oh look at me! Look at me! Look how fancy I am! I'm a crook! And no one knows it! La dee da dee da!*"

"I was *never* a hero, boy. Everything I own – *everything* – is stolen. These sheets. Those shoes. Everything!"

"Not everything!"

"*Everything.*"

"Your cab?"

"Stolen."

"The dogs?"

"Stolen – from a priest."

"Even this bell?"

"Stolen twice. Stole it. Gave it to a duchess. Stole it back. It's a problem, I admit."

"It doesn't matter. No one just makes up a Rottweiler. It has to come from somewhere deep inside. I think it just got buried under – I don't know – a lot of rotten garbage, it seems to me."

"Are you done?"

"No! Come on! Let's go! Let's go rescue –"

"Go back to bed."

"Come on!"

"I'll call my men –"

"Oh, they can't touch me! I'm much smarter than they are."

He stared at me sideways.

"Then stay," he said. "Stay right there. Shout all you want. It makes no difference to me."

And with that, he tipped over onto his side and fell fast asleep. I shouted and jumped and kicked at him, but it was no use. He was dead to the world. Still, my mission was clear. I had found the crack in his armor.

I would reform The Rottweiler.

For the next few days I was relentless. At every opportunity I chided and nagged him. Each time, he'd have his men cart me off and lock me up, and each time I laughed and returned. To his astonishment, no room in his house could hold me. (And locking me out of the house didn't work either.) And after three days, he called me to his study. There, he and Woolsy waited, pacing the room.

"Boy, I've had just about enough of you," he said.

"Yes, sir."

"You've taxed my patience. If I thought I could keep you out of the house, I'd've locked you out days ago."

"Yes, sir."

"But the fact is, as much as I could give a fig what's happened to the man, I've decided to… extend some of my feelers. Purely on a whim."

"Yes, sir. And?"

"My dear friend Squinty has suggested that useful information may be gained this very evening at Red's Alley."

"Red's Alley, sir?"

"Yes, it's league night. There's likely to be quite a lot of action. Woolsy and I were just readying to leave."

"Wonderful! I'm coming, too," I said. "You may need me!"

"I think not," he said. "The only reason I told you was –"

"Filial obligation?"

"– to stop you picking my locks! You've ruined half the doors on my house, boy! They don't grow on trees!"

"Sorry, sir."

Then Sir Roderick and Woolsy packed up their service revolvers and were gone. I feigned going back to the stables and hid myself on the back of their cab, where I stayed, undetected.

After twenty minutes or so, we drove onto a seamy, deserted street on the lower east side, and parked outside "Red's Alley," a tavern. Sir Roderick and Woolsy went inside. I snuck around to observe from the side window.

When Sir Roderick spoke of an "alley," I didn't take him literally – but that's exactly what it was: a ten-pin alley with some 30 lanes and – to my astonishment – every bowler inside – no matter how grungy or grotesque – had a shock of scarlet hair. A huge, scrawled sign on the side wall read: *Thursday Night – Red Headed Bowling League! (Beer half-price.)*

Sir Roderick and Woolsy – no strangers to this midnight world – clearly knew all of the men, and wasted no time carousing. Eventually, they were brought to a back room where a giant, orange-haired man with a white apron was carrying an immense barrel. I assumed this was Red. He was none too keen to hear Sir Roderick's questions, and for a moment, it looked as if a fight might break out. But Sir Roderick calmed him down and Red started talking. After listening intently, they bid him goodbye and went back to the cab. A moment later we were bustling towards the waterfront.

"Well?" I said, sticking my head down through the opening in the carriage, half scaring them both to death.

"Boy!" shouted Sir Roderick, enraged.

"What did you learn?"

"I learned my bowling team can't last five minutes without me," muttered Woolsy.

"About Holmes!?" I said.

"According to Red," said Sir Roderick, "Holmes was last seen at a docking warehouse owned by one A. Troy."

"Another A!" said Woolsy.

"No relation," I said.

"Well, I nicked Red's directory," continued Woolsy.

"Good man," said Sir Roderick.

"It lists the owner as 'Arim Troy'."

"Arim Troy. Arim Troy. Now, why does that sound so terribly familiar?"

"Could it be –?" started Woolsy.

"Yeeesss?" said Sir Roderick, patiently.

"Perhaps –?" continued Woolsy.

"Go on," said Sir Roderick.

"Aaahmmm –?" continued Woolsy.

Sir Roderick stared at him, stupidly.

"...Never mind," said Woolsy.

"Right. Well, we'll know soon enough," countered Sir Roderick.

It invigorated me to see Sir Roderick seemingly back in his element and on a case. As we approached the waterfront, he ordered the cab to halt several hundred yards from the warehouse, so as not to attract attention.

"If Holmes really is here," said Sir Roderick, "we may not have much time. Woolsy, we'll cover more ground splitting up. Keep your revolver cocked. Boy – *stay in the cab!*"

"But – yes, sir," I said.

I watched as the two circled to opposite sides of the building. As soon as they were out of sight, I left the cab and trailed after Sir Roderick. From a darkened alcove, I watched him approach the edge of the pier, near the back of the warehouse. A thin, lean, bent-over, white-haired figure was directing half a dozen brawny workers to carry boxes onto a ship docked nearby.

As Sir Roderick approached them, a look of excitement grew upon his face.

"Arim Troy, indeed! Ahoy there!" he cried.

The men turned toward him, alarmed.

"*Professor Moriarty, I presume?*"

Moriarty?! It couldn't be! No one had *ever* seen the man before. Yet he was rumored far and wide as Sherlock Holmes' greatest arch-nemesis and the most notorious criminal genius in all London, perhaps even the world! If this was Moriarty, surely Sir Roderick was placing himself in grave, grave peril.

But he was acting like a schoolboy!

"Who wants to know?" asked the old man. And then, he took a closer look at Sir Roderick. "Why, you're that pretty boy with the dog's name from *The Straggler*, aren't you? And wandering the docks alone at night? That can't be safe. My dear boy, I daresay, you may have made a mistake tonight."

And then, looking at his men, Moriarty said, "Kill him."

My heart froze. Sir Roderick was easily outnumbered. Yet he seemed *gleeful!*

"Oh no no no no no no no!" laughed Sir Roderick. "You misunderstand! I've been dying to meet you!"

Moriarty and his men exchanged befuddled looks.

"Napoleon of Crime! Master of the Underworld!" Sir Roderick continued. "Criminal Genius! This is – I'm sorry if I'm getting a bit – emotional! – I thought you were a myth!"

I couldn't believe what I was seeing. It was too much.

"You're my *hero!*" said Sir Roderick, and he seemed absolutely sincere.

"Professor?" called one of the men. "Should we kill him?"

"Hold," said Moriarty.

"Professor," said another, "That there's The Rottweiler! The second greatest –"

"I know who he is, dolt!"

"He's put dozens of our men away!"

"Silence!" said Moriarty.

"Oh, no, no!" said Sir Roderick. "Don't you see? None of those men went to jail – or not for very long at any rate! No! That was *my scheme!* See, I'm a criminal genius, too! Just like you! Well, not on par with you, of course – but –"

From my hiding spot I saw that I had placed too much faith in Sir Roderick's change of heart. And now, I'd driven him straight to the criminal underworld's lord and master!

"He arrested Squinty, Black Jack, and that bloke that makes bombs," said another thug.

"The 'Bomb-Making Guy' is his preferred appellation," said Sir Roderick. "And honestly, we're all buddies! Just ask them! Ask the Butcher Street Semi-Irregulars!"

"I read he just recovered the stolen crown jewels," said another hood.

"And *kept them*, thank you!" said The Rottweiler, proudly.

"Did you?" Moriarty said, intrigued. "Where?"

"Ah…well…that is to say…" stumbled Sir Roderick.

One of the hoods aimed his firearm directly at Sir Roderick, and cocked the trigger.

"442D Butcher Street. Second floor."

"Aars, Gustav," said Moriarty. "Search the place. See if he's telling the truth."

The two men disappeared. Then Moriarty leveled his own pistol at Sir Roderick.

"So, you commit crimes and then solve them, eh?"

"Right! Now, you've got it."

"Interesting, if it's true," said Moriarty. "I first thought you might be here for another reason."

"Oh no!"

"You just happened to be wandering the docks alone at night. Armed."

Moriarty snatched Sir Roderick's sidearm from inside his coat.

"And accompanied by your most trusted ally. Also armed."

From the corner of the dock, Colonel Woolsy was pushed forward, surrounded by more of Moriarty's goons.

"Woolsy..." lamented Sir Roderick.

"Tell me," said Moriarty. "Of all your myriad 'crimes' – do you count among them – *murder?*"

"Murder? Oh – well – of course! What criminal genius doesn't murder? I murder – sometimes two – three – four times before breakfast!"

"I see," said Moriarty, a devilish leer rising upon his face. "Let's test that mettle then, shall we?"

He turned and nodded at two of his men.

"Take 'The Rottweiler' to Room 21B and tie the other one up here. Be quick! There's work to be done."

The two hoods led Sir Roderick into the warehouse at gunpoint, while I followed at a safe distance. When we arrived at Room 21B, I remained outside, peering in through a crack in the doorway. Inside, the tiny gray room was dimly lit and there sat a solitary man tied to a chair. His head hung low as if he'd been severely hurt. As I looked closer, I saw the figure stir, and finally lift his head. And then I saw him, clearly. *The man in the chair was Holmes.*

"Good Lord," said Sir Roderick, astonished.

Slowly, painfully, the bound detective whispered, "*Help me...*"

"Do it," said the hood directly behind Sir Roderick, forcing a revolver into his hand.

Sir Roderick turned back to the captive detective. I couldn't believe what I was seeing. I knew Sir Roderick disliked Holmes, but this was too much. And it was *my fault!* I had forced him to come here! Brought him to this very spot! What could I do?! My grief was unbearable.

Sir Roderick leveled the revolver at Holmes and girded himself. His hand trembled as he cocked the gun. Sweat collected on his brow. But – it was no use. His shoulders collapsed. His head dropped in shame.

"I can't," he said. "I – can't."

"Of course, you can't," came a whisper. "You can't – because you're weak –!"

But who was speaking? It was...it was *Holmes!* Holmes, who, a moment ago was on the verge of collapse. Now, he was looking up, leering and grinning, *evilly*. It was too much! Sir Roderick stared, aghast.

"Criminal genius?" Holmes laughed. And then he stood up. The ropes that bound him dropped like loose string.

"You're no criminal genius," he said. "I should know!"

And with that, Holmes tore the hair from his own head, removed a nose that was putty and peeled off heavy furrowed eyebrows. Now, standing before us once again, was *Moriarty!* My heart froze.

"Commit crimes and then solve them, do you?!
You can't imagine you're the first 'criminal genius'
who ever thought of that?!"

"*You* are Holmes?" stammered Sir Roderick.

Moriarty laughed.

"Stay back!" said Sir Roderick, lifting his
revolver, again.

"You can't think I'd actually provide you with a
loaded weapon," he grinned.

Suddenly, a short, sharp smile appeared across
The Rottweiler's face.

"Who said it wasn't loaded?"

All color fled from Moriarty's face. With
lightning-like reflexes, he lunged at Sir Roderick just
as the gun fired. Sir Roderick's shot shattered the
room's one lightbulb, encasing them all in absolute
darkness.

"Now, boy!" he called, and frantically, I leapt in.

Of course, I was no match for the larger men, but I
knew well enough where they were, and it was easy to
trip them into one another. Nearby, a struggle went
on between The Rottweiler and Moriarty and a pair of
shots rang out. A moment later, a wounded body –
Moriarty's – lurched out of the room and down the
corridor.

"Sir Roderick!" I cried.

"I'm fine, boy. Come on!"

We moved into the hallway, bracing the door
behind us.

"You've been shot!"

"Grazed. He got the worst of it. And he'll have a
nice surprise waiting for him back at the docks."

Giving him my arm, we hurried back to the entrance.

"You *knew* Holmes was Moriarty?"

"I suspected. The moment he said he wanted to 'test' me. I had a feeling it involved Holmes – and had Holmes and Moriarty been true rivals, I knew Moriarty would have never kept him alive so long. When I saw Holmes tied to the chair, I assumed it was Moriarty – and therefore knew the gun he gave me couldn't be loaded."

"But how did you get the bullets?!"

But The Rottweiler merely grinned at me.

In a minute, we were out of the warehouse – and in the middle of a dockyard fracas! Squinty, Red and number of men from the bowling alley had engaged Moriarty's men and were overpowering them. Nearby, a freed Woolsy guided two snarling Rottweilers to assist our men.

"There!" cried Sir Roderick.

Sure enough, Moriarty, bleeding heavily at the shoulder, was lowering a gunny sack from the pier to a small boat on the water. The Rottweiler ran over, pulled him up, knocked the gun from his hand and started thrashing him. Looking quickly for a weapon, Moriarty found a massive dock worker's hook and started slashing with it. A lucky strike knocked The Rottweiler to the ground, and Moriarty stood over him, a maniacal look on his face, about to administer the killing blow. Without thinking, I reached for the only object I had on me, Sir Roderick's gold bell and flung it with all my strength at Moriarty. It wasn't enough to hurt him – but the sound and impact distracted him – time enough for The Rottweiler to lash Moriarty's own hook into his wounded shoulder, throwing him backwards off the pier, and into the water.

We ran to the edge and looked, but the river was a murky black – with no sign of Moriarty.

"Do you think –?"

"I doubt it," said Sir Roderick. "His kind never stays down for good."

"His kind?" I said. "Don't you mean *your* kind?"

The Rottweiler looked at me, surprised. But before he could answer, the sound of police sirens filled the air. The pier hoodlums scattered. The Rottweiler gave a sign of thanks to Squinty and Red, who departed quickly. What few men remained of Moriarty's were rounded up by the police.

"Chief Inspector!" called a policeman nearby. He held up Moriarty's gunny sack. "It's true! Moriarty had the true crown jewels all along!"

"You see?" said The Rottweiler.

"Well! Good show!" said the Chief Inspector. "Too bad Holmes still seems to be missing!"

"Yes, it's a damn shame," said Sir Roderick, as he and Woolsy quietly grinned at one another.

"So much," muttered Woolsy, under his breath, "for the competition…"

"In-deed," said Sir Roderick.

Next morning, I ate breakfast in the Great Hall at Sir Roderick's dining table for the very first time. He seemed extremely pleased.

"You're not upset about losing the jewels?" I asked.

"If I know Scotland Yard, I doubt they'll keep them long," he said. "And you're not upset, boy, that you may have just ended the career of the world's greatest detective?"

"On the contrary, sir," I said. "I believe I just helped start it!"

I devoured the ham and eggs on my plate, feeling every bit the king.

"Don't get used to it, boy," said The Rottweiler. "You're still sleeping with the dogs."

And, at that moment, I didn't even mind.

Somewhere Other than Earth

SPACE. A tiny, 1950's-era, Buster Crabbe-type rocket vaults through the cosmos.

BOOMING NARRATOR: Fleeing from an Earth overrun by digital madness, Mark Savage and his pal, Dani, wander the stars in their two-person rocket, Chanticleer! Their destination: *Somewhere Other Than Earth!*

A DENSE JUNGLE. MARK and DANI – in space outfits – make their way through a clearing. Suddenly, they're ambushed by four ferocious monsters: GORGO, RODAN, MOTHRA and KONG. All carry little electronic devices.

RODAN: Humans!!!

MARK: We come in peace!

The monsters circle them, warily.

DANI: Is this the Planet of Flying Rat Warriors?

MARK: Is it the Bad Hair Planet?

KONG: No! This is the Planet Where Everyone's Writing an e-Book!

The monsters wave their electronic devices.

OTHERS: Read mine! Read mine!

DANI: But we just left a planet like that!

RODAN: Read mine! It's a cross between *The Fault in Our Stars* and *Fight Club!*

MOTHRA: Mine is totally lendable!

RODAN: Mine has 18 likes on Goodreads!

GORGO: Mine is free with a subscription to (*squawking untranslatably*) EEEAARY AAROKA!!! Or Amazon Prime.

Mark whips out his ray-gun.

MARK: Alright! Get back!

Dani sees something on the ground. She points, frightened.

DANI: Mark! Tiny intelligent bugs with Nooks!

The Monsters stomp on the bugs, aggressively.

MARK: Stop! Stop! Oh God! Are you *all* such desperate authors!?

MOTHRA: I work in non-franchise, locavore coffee shop!

RODAN: I'm a licensed yoga instructor!

Kong thumps his chest.

KONG: And where are *your* e-books?!

MARK: We left them on Earth! We're trying to get away from all that!

The monsters move towards them, ferociously. Thinking quickly, Dani, whips something out of her pocket.

DANI: Wait! We have these!

Kong grabs them, examines them.

KONG: Indecipherable plot points – on napkins!

MOTHRA: This one's on – Kindle stationery!

The monsters fall to the ground, humbling themselves.

RODAN: Forgive us!

GORGO: We were rude!

KONG: Please review my book! I will eat your encmies!

MOTHRA: Review my book!

OTHERS: No, mine! Mine!

The enraged monsters begin battling amongst themselves.

MARK (*to Dani*): Come on!

They run off. Gorgo examines the napkins.

GORGO: Hey! Hey! This is good! This works!

Everyone freezes.

BOOMING NARRATOR: Where will Mark and Dani find themselves next?! *Somewhere Other Than Earth!*

The Raglan Oracle

Christmas last year will not be a day that I – or anyone in my family – will soon forget, I dare say. I write this comfortably from a bed at my Aunt Sara's house. As you know, we did not make it to Sara's last year. And we were anything but comfortable. The storms and snow of last year were greater than any we'd seen in decades. And while that would not usually stop my daddy from makin' the trip, Ethan, as you know, was quite sick.

Poor Ethan – all of four years – had been a fairly strong boy till that last year – when various sickness overtook him. I had been packing an overnight bag for the trip up north when my Uncle Campbell told me that Ethan was burning up and we'd have to stay put. Daddy had gone for the doctor – a half-day trip, at the least. Ma was in her bedroom laying compresses on Ethan. His fever was high.

Over the past few years, my family had fallen into something of an isolation from the rest of the town, as tends to happen with farming families. Arguments are started and never resolved. Families lose touch and keep to themselves. And so, the begrudging offer to visit from my Aunt was quickly discarded when Ethan fell ill. Soon, a pallor lay over our house as wind crept in through chipped planks causing a low, solemn whistle. The holiday tree I'd cut down myself stood bent over, unseasonable.

Our town, Raglan, is a small one. There aren't but forty, fifty families – all of whom I can name by sight.

There's little crime, no jail, and half the townsfolk can't write or read proper. In fact, a great many, in this year of our lord 1873, still believe Lincoln runs the capital, if you can believe that.

Which may be why Ethan's sickness – and his babbling in particular – came off so unsettling.

I was the one heard it first. I had woken up early that morning to his kicking and writhing. Still asleep, but tossing, turning. And saying words over and over that I couldn't understand:

Nixon

Nixon

Nixon meant nothing to me or ma. It was simply a nonsense word for which we had no particular reference. It was Uncle Cam, who had been a profuse reader and was teaching me to write proper, who said that it sounded like something out of *Alice* – a book he'd seen at the general store – that was full of its own strange puzzles. Cam was the one who had started listening closely to Ethan, like what he was saying might actually mean something.

At first, he thought *Nixon* might be a city or a port. But of course, we had no map to look on. Our curiosities about Ethan's poor fortune did not exactly sit well with my ma, and we made efforts to keep our thoughts to ourselves. But that afternoon, after my mother fell asleep rocking him, Cam and I began takin' notes of his babbling.

Nixon

Leaks

Plumbers

Our roof leaked, and Cam had heard of "plumbers" back east. As my mother slept, Cam whispered gently to my poor brother to expand on his phrases.

"Boy – what is *Nixon*?"

"Ask about the water sluice, Uncle Cam," I whispered.

"It's not a sluice," he brayed at me. "He said it's a – gate."

"Ask him."

"Ethan," Cam whispered, "what is the *water gate*?"

Ethan tossed back and forth, "*re-elect – re-elect –*"

"Re-elect who?" whispered Uncle Cam, mesmerized.

"*Re-elect...the president.*"

"Grant?"

"*The President –*" said Ethan.

"We did," Cam said. "Grant *was* re-elected!"

"*Nixon*," moaned Ethan. "*Re-elect Nixon.*" His quaking woke up my mother.

"Leave him be!" she scolded.

We removed ourselves to the outer room. Cam's eyes were afire. He studied our notes.

"What's wrong with him, Uncle Cam? What's *Nixon*?"

"Not what boy. *Who*. And only the President of the United States, I'd reckon."

"Before Grant –?"

"Oh no. *After.*"

My eyes went wide.

"Boy, there's *never* been a President Nixon. Not *ever*. So, who is he? A made-up name? D'you know anyone named 'Nixon'? Your family ever met anyone –"

"Not that I –"

"'Course not. Even if you did, that boy's only four. He couldn't possible remember anyone with that name. Which means what he's sayin' is either utter nonsense. Or –"

"Or what?"

"*Or he's telling the future.*"

I stared at Cam, stunned.

"I've read of this. People in trances – taught to see things other than what's really there –"

"But nobody's told him nothing. He's just sick."

"Don't ask me to explain it. In a boy like Ethan – who knows what a fever's unlocked?"

Cam was excited, but I could only think of my little brother in pain, overcome by some demon.

"Will he be okay?" I asked.

Cam looked at me, blankly, the thrill drained from his face. He knelt beside me.

"'Course he will! 'Course he will! Bless that boy! You know you two are the best things ever happened to your daddy and Mary. You listen to me. Your daddy'll be back with that doctor and they'll take care of things. I promise."

Cam's words encouraged me. From my mother's bedroom Ethan groaned: *Agnew*

Cam pressed the paper and pencil into my hand.

"Here! Stay helpful to your ma – and keep takin' notes. Maybe it's delirium. Or maybe he does know something."

"Like what?"

"Like maybe this 'Nixon' is going to be president. Maybe the *next* president."

Cam grabbed his coat and headed to the door.

"Where're you going?"

"To McCall's, to think this through. And remember – this is just between you and me! So, don't upset your ma."

And Uncle Cam was gone. After two hours at McCall's, more likely than not, he wouldn't even remember *Nixon*. But now, somethin' was roused in me. Despite a gross burden of shame, I gave in to shiftless curiosity. Folding the paper neatly into my pocket, I went to help watch over Ethan, but secretly took notes as ma changed and cleaned his linens.

Two hours later, daddy still hadn't returned, and Ethan was more restless than ever. Ma rushed about, frantically switching between cooling him down, keeping our fire lit and prayer.

Uncle Cam returned, drenched in a staleness of beer and accompanied by Morton, a stocky farmer, and Bridwell, a shopkeeper. All came in, respectful, removing their hats. Bridwell had brown-paper-wrapped meats and coffee, and presented them graciously to my mother.

"Heard about the boy. Terrible news. Awful way to spend Christmas. Anything we or the wives can do – you tell us."

"That's kind of you, Charlie."

"Is he awake?" asked Morton, meekly.

"No, he's sleeping," said my mother.

The men looked at each other.

"Thank goodness," they agreed.

Bridwell helped ma take the packages to the kitchen. Uncle Cam and Mr. Morton quickly took me aside.

"Well, what's he said? Have you got anything?"

"I thought this was between us?"

"It is! This is just Morton! Bridwell! Neighbors!"

He knelt beside me.

"Now, boy – news like this, we need more minds to reflect on."

"But just these two? That's it?"

"I solemnly swear."

Mr. Morton peered down at me, his breath as sour as Cam's.

"Let spill, son. What've you got?"

I withdrew my notes.

"As I can make it out, he's said: *Krogh, Colson, Hunt.* He called them *plumbers.* He said: *Creep.* All part of *creep…*"

The men looked at each other, perplexed.

"Like creeping around?" said Morton.

"Sounded to me like more of a group," I said. "Like that was the name of their club."

"Ah," said Cam. "It's an organization. That's what I said!"

"That's what *I* said!" said Bridwell, rejoining us.

There was a slam at the front door as my daddy and the doctor – a burly man – came in, covered with snow.

"Where is he?" The doctor demanded.

"In the bedroom," said Cam. The two men went in, while the others returned their attention to me.

"*Gray destroys evidence. Liddy. Cover up.* He said that one an awful lot – *Cover up. Cover up.* Ma kept putting blankets on him, but he kept sayin' it. He said – *Nixon knew* – and *Cox resigns* –"

Morton leaned in.

"There's a Wilfred Cox in Langston! He's a congressman."

"He's *postmaster,*" corrected Bridwell.

"Same thing," barked Morton.

"This next part," I said, "I didn't really understand. *Tapes*, he said. *Missing tapes.* Said it a few times. An' then he quieted down."

The men looked at each other.

"Measuring tape?"

"What would he need measuring tape for?"

Bridwell stepped away from us, glaring.

"Confound it, Campbell! You drag us three miles in blistering snow –"

"Lower your voice!" said Cam. He looked at me, helpless.

"I don't think it was for measuring," I said, fumbling through my notes.

Morton grabbed the paper from me, remembered he couldn't read and passed it to my uncle. I pointed to a scrawled line.

"Something about – *recordings* – and they're – they're missing –"

"Harrumph" went Bridwell.

"Maybe these tapes are like – newspapers," I started, "Maybe they were recording their conversations and –"

"*Of course,*" cried Cam. "You see what this means?!"

We all looked at him, confused.

"Scandal!"

"*Scandal?*" the other men gasped.

I didn't follow the implication, but Bridwell and Morton were now staring as wildly as Cam.

"Of the highest order! This man – this *Nixon* – president-to-be – becomes implicated in some – some *cover-up*. That's what he means. Right, boy?! Not that he was *cold?*"

"Maybe," I answered.

"He keeps some journal – some recording of their conversation – and this Cox finds it! And turns it in! To the papers! The authorities! And then – *scandal!*"

"You think so?" asked Bridwell.

"Has to be," said Uncle. "It's all there."

"But who are these people?!" asked Morton.

"They're from the future, Ben!"

"Unbelievable!" said Bridwell. "It's too fantastic!"

From the bedroom a creaky voice called:

Ziegler

Kissinger

Impeachment

"*Impeachment!*" the men echoed.

"We must go to the boy!" said Morton. "We have to hear more!"

Suddenly, a thin banshee's wail issued from the room, and then, just as quick, the house fell silent. The doctor came back out.

"How is he?" asked Morton.

"Sick," said the doctor. "He needs as much rest as possible."

"Of course," said Bridwell.

"I gave him something to sleep."

"You what?!" Morton blurted.

The doctor looked at them, perplexed. Cam stepped forward.

"Good. Good. Everything for the best. We've been quite worried."

The doctor eyed them, suspiciously, pulled his coat on.

"Strangest babbling."

"Will he – babble later?" Bridwell interrupted.

"Now, see here," said the doctor, glaring at them. "What're the three of you on about?!"

The men exchanged a glance.

"Alright, Doc," started Cam. "What do you know about *tapes*?"

Within hours of the doctor's departure, the word had gotten out, and our house had become a place of pilgrimage. By ten-thirty, despite the harsh weather, some forty people had come and gone. Some were sincerely concerned with Ethan's health and expressed their sympathies to his suffering. But many had intentions not so respectable.

Despite the size of the crowd, my folks seemed ignorant of their true reasons for coming. And this surprised me, as everyone following the story had developed highly complex opinions which they had great difficulty keeping to themselves.

"*Ford?!* He named Ford vice-president?! That bumbler!"

"Had to! *Agnew resigned!*"

"He was appointed! That Nixon could've picked anybody!"

"He should've appointed Kissinger!"

"Kissinger's not American!"

"Have they impeached him, yet?"

"Not yet! Anytime now!"

"Has he said what year it is!?"

"It's 1899 – he said –"

"He didn't say that! He hasn't said what year yet!"

"It's got to be later! Turn of the century!"

"Three dollars says its 1902!"

"I'll take that bet!"

"And what on earth is *Viet Nam?*"

Most folks brought food. Many brought wreaths and decorations and a few decent types brought gifts. My mother – oblivious to the conversations – took comfort from the crowd. My aunts Min and Sara came – the three women having fallen out over raspberry pie disagreements some two-odd years ago. And there was tree trimming, laughter and drink, disrupted occasionally, by the reminder that we were all here because a small boy was suffering.

By the end of the evening what few people were left had either renewed friendships with my folks or were plain snoopers, waiting for Ethan's story's proper conclusion.

It was early the next morning when the doctor stepped out of my mother's room and rustled my daddy awake. All remaining guests lay asleep on chairs and the floor.

"Fever's broke," the doctor whispered.

"The boy –?" asked my father.

"Fine," said the doctor. "He'll be fine."

"He's sleeping," added my mother, coming out of the room and locking the door. "He's peaceful. Won't be any babbling anymore."

The doctor buttoned up his coat and left. Bridwell and Morton, dazed, got to their feet. They looked at my mother.

"Did he – did he –" Morton stuttered.

"Did he *say anything?*" Bridwell asked.

"Did they –?"

"Impeach Nixon?" asked my mother. "No. He resigned."

"*Resigned?*"

"*Before* they could impeach him. Yes," she said, smiling at me.

"Did he ever give a year?"

"Not that I recall," said my mother.

"Hmph. Well," said Bridwell, getting his coat. "The important thing –"

"Yes," said my mother. "The boy is fine. Thank you."

She took Mr. Bridwell's scarf and affectionately wrapped it around his neck, and then led our neighbors to the door.

"You two get home safe," she said.

And they were gone, leaving only me, my family and Uncle Cam, snoring soundly on the floor.

"Who's Nixon?" asked my daddy.

"No one, dear," said my mother. "No one important."

And she came over and covered me with a blanket and kissed me. She stoked the fire and, watching her, I drifted peacefully into a deep, sound sleep.

All the Comforts

"Oooooh!" *"Ahhh!"* *"Glaav!"*

Murmurs of awe erupted from 96 passengers, encompassing eight different planetary species, and 18 languages, as yet another "Moment of Wonder" appeared outside the southern window of *Gerrison's Interstellar Adventure Macrobuus*. This time, it was tiny pin-pop flashes of phosphate crackling in the early morning light against the dark red background of Mt. Dosav'a on the lushly popular planet Jove8.

Of the 96 passengers, only three did not *Oooooh Ahhh or Glaav*. They were: Colcalm, the bus-driver, who's sacred trust was to simply keep his eyes on the road; Merrieux, the young, golden, half-Jovian/half-French tour guide who, while still taken by the light show, remained a consummate professional; and Dick Magrish, 82-year-old human from Budweiser, Michigan, NAmerica, Sol3 (Earth), who continuously wore a sleep mask and earplugs during every highlight of the tour.

Over the past three days, most of the passengers had grown to hate Dick, including his own species, Sol3 Homo Sapiens. They hated Dick because he was old, smelled bad, and seemed angry all the time. But mostly they hated him because he refused to socialize with them. When they stopped for mid-day or evening feeding sessions, he remained on the bus or sat alone, separately. When they went to view an exhibit, or experience the local nightlife, he merely grunted and retired to his sleep cell. And if they ever pestered him for conversation, he'd bark at them *back off! Stay Away!* or *Git!*

Outside of luggage, sleep mask, and earplugs, Dick appeared to carry only three things with him: a thermos of decaf coffee, a bakery bag containing that day's stale cinnamon roll and a battered, 25-year-old racing form.

He dreamt of vipers, slithering, spitting, and coiling around his neck. He tugged up his mask, and was startled to see a real viper – or almost – it was a small, *Caresian* boy – a purple, scaly toddler with split tongue and narrow eyes.

"Hey! Hey!" said Dick, recoiling in revulsion.

"Shhmellsh shhweet," said the boy, pointing at Dick's bakery bag.

Dick gripped the bag, protectively, against his chest.

"Get outta here!" he said, waving the boy off.

The passengers glared at him.

"O-kay, bye," said the boy, generously. And he returned to his family.

Dick sank into his seat. Today was the final day of the tour. A few more hours and it would all be over.

Mid-afternoon.

"No!" repeated Dick, over and over, as Merrieux held the translucent de-breather near his mouth.

"I would remind Monsieur," she said, "that he signed an agreement to use the de-breather when necessary. Until Monsieur wears the de-breather the bus cannot go forward."

The last leg of the trip was 120 miles through a pure methane atmosphere. The bus itself actually purified 99.867% of the air into nicely breathable oxygen (for those that required it). But after several years of protest and litigation, new regulations required all passengers to don de-breathers as appropriate.

Make 'im wear the goddamn de-breather! shouted diverse languages. *Kick him off the bus!* yelled a female made entirely of rocks.

Dick gnawed on his cinnamon roll.

"May I remind Monsieur," said Merrieux, ever polite, "that he has already had two warnings regarding the de-breather. With a third warning, I am authorized to remove Monsieur from the bus at my discretion. However, in six years, I have only ever removed two passengers. I would prefer not to spoil that record."

Dick said nothing, gripped his seat handles.

"Does Monsieur wish to leave the adventure bus?"

Slowly, Dick lifted the de-breather to his face and clamped it on. Merrieux patted him gently and moved down the aisle. Dick leaned his head back and pulled his sleep mask on.

Hours later.

"Monsieur? Monsieur? We are here."

Dick pulled the mask down, and unclamped the de-breather, as Merrieux disembarked, leaving him alone on the deserted bus. From outside the window, colored lights flickered and danced. Thermos and bakery bag in hand, Dick made his way off the vehicle.

They had arrived at K'lyn K'rayva – the legendary *Gates of Heaven*. The crowd of passengers had assembled at the front of a sweeping observation deck and were watching as far off Mt. V'anno spewed neon, lava fireworks into the translucent blue of K'rayva's lake, only to be immediately extinguished by the triplet, sister waterfalls – Anaya, Na'am, and N'agari. Color and warmth pulsated as life forms from eight planets and cultures stood as one, enraptured.

Dick, careful to ensure that no one was paying any attention to him, wandered to the far, right edge of the observation deck, climbed over the guardrail, and up onto the embankment. He ascended a butte of rocks, where Anaya sprayed him like an angry goddess. He sat upon a wet crag, nestled his thermos and bakery bag into his lap, and withdrew the golden sphere from his jacket pocket.

"I'm sorry, Maggie," he said. "I'm so sorry. I know I said *no* too much. But I got you here. Finally."

He stared out at what even he had to admit was an astonishingly beautiful view.

"Well," he said, "you were right, Maggie. It does remind me of you."

He unscrewed the golden sphere, exposing the sheer, white powder. And then he shook the powder into Anaya. And when the powder was all gone, he closed the sphere and threw it into Anaya.

And then his world was over.

And after a moment, he became conscious of a small, purple, snake-like boy sitting next to him, staring, like him, out at the water.

"Itsh pretty," said the boy.

"Yes, it is," said Dick.

And he opened his bag and tore off a piece of cinnamon roll and shared it with the boy. And they sat there, together, eating and basking in the warmth and color.

Dr. Downey

"I don't like Dr. Russell," said Mrs. Epstein. "There's something off about him!"

Dr. Paula Downey, 63, the Co-Head of the Physical Therapy Unit at Hillside Medical smiled, nodded, and continued gently manipulating Candy Epstein's tender, arthritic right leg. Candace, a sweet, nosy octogenarian, had had a relatively mild dust-up with three other cars on the parkway six months ago. After her initial recovery period, she had come to Dr. Downey for weekly therapy sessions. Except for the brittleness of age, her injury was relatively mild – but her weekly therapy sessions – which included stretching, pulling, complaining about pains, getting weekly meds and generally dishing the dirt – had become the highlight of her week.

Today was a difficult day, though, for Mrs. Epstein. Not because of nagging leg pain, but because it was Dr. Downey's last at Hillside. She was retiring early.

"He has that goatee," Mrs. Epstein continued. "And I'm not the only one who thinks he's strange. Half your patients think something's seriously wrong with him."

"Really?" said Dr. Downey, trying not to seem amused.

"And –" she continued, deftly, "I saw him in the parking lot the other day with your receptionist –"

"Beth?"

"Yes. And he was acting very unprofessional!"

Dr. Downey continued stretching her leg. She imagined, after six months that she knew this leg at least as well as she knew the woman attached to it.

"And I don't like that he's forcing you out!" Mrs. Epstein asserted. "It's sexism! Age-ism!"

"He's not forcing me out. I made the choice to retire on my own. And really, I think once you get to know him –"

"I don't *want* to know him! Will you please just – I don't know – Google his background – or have somebody look into him?"

"Mrs. Epstein, you know very well, Dr. Russell was thoroughly vetted by the Board months ago," she paused, then leaned close to Mrs. Epstein and added, "but between us? Yes, he is *extremely creepy*."

"See?! You see what I mean?!"

"I'll Google him. I promise."

Mrs. Epstein smiled, relieved. The doctor shifted her leg.

"All right, let's work on that left knee."

They worked the sore knee another five minutes. Then, tearing up a bit, Mrs. Epstein turned from her.

"What will we do without you?" she bit her lip, shivering. "So many of us rely on you!"

"Mrs. Epstein – please. You'll make me cry. Look," she said, taking one of her brand-new business cards off of her desk and pressing it firmly, comfortingly into Mrs. Epstein's palm. "If you're really in such awful shape, call me. All right?"

"Thank you. Thank you. And –"

"Yes?"

"Well – about my – my meds –"

"Mrs. Epstein, I think you've finished your course."

"Yes. I know. But – I could use – just a few more. While you're still here?"

Downey looked at her, reprovingly, opened a nearby cabinet and withdrew a packet of pills. She handed them to Mrs. Epstein, who gripped them, tightly.

"Now," said the doctor, "I'm sure I don't have to remind you of our arrangement?"

"Of course! Payment on delivery," giggled Mrs. Epstein. "Would you hand me my bag?"

She gave the bag to Mrs. Epstein who withdrew a bulky, manila envelope and handed it to her. The doctor matter-of-factly set it inside a large cardboard packing box on the floor.

"Thirty thousand," said Mrs. Epstein. "It's all there."

"I'm sure," said Downey. And then she whispered to her, like a schoolgirl sharing a secret. "And you kept this just between us? Because we don't want any trouble –!"

"Heavens, no! You know I could never have afforded these if you hadn't gotten them from – from – *Canada?*"

"Yes," replied Dr. Downey. "Canada."

Outside, the waiting room was packed with men and women, all in their late 80's and 90's, all looking hopeless and destitute. Many were arthritic and hunched over, and some of them few quivered and shook. One thing in common – they all carried largish purses, bags, or bulky manila envelopes, similar to Mrs. Epstein's, on their laps.

Posters and charts around the waiting room illustrated the benefits of good movement, posture, and stretching. Beth, Dr. Downey's young receptionist, played a dot-connecting game on her iPhone, and chewed gum. Mrs. Epstein, smiling but tearful, waddled across the room and to the exit. Downey stepped into the room, took the measure of her population, and read from a clipboard.

"Mrs. Glick?" she said.

Mrs. Glick, a woman in a curly, blue steel wig, in her early 90's, lifted the large bulky purse from her lap and hobbled towards Dr. Downey's examination room.

The day drew to a close. Dr. Downey packed up her office for the final time, placing stacks of hidden, bundled cash into her black, mid-sized suitcase. She balanced a large box of certificates atop the suitcase and wheeled it into the now empty waiting room. Beth, putting things away for the night, came out from behind reception and hugged her, affectionately.

"Are you headed straight for Florida?" she asked.

"I think I'm going to spend some time in the islands, first," said Dr. Downey.

The doctor came out into the cool night air of the parking lot, and loaded the suitcase and box into her car.

She looked back at the center, and reflected on how warmly she'd come to feel about all the patients, despite the fact that she'd only been there half a year. Certainly, she had held positions for far less time than this one. And she had grown to like being "Dr. Downey, Dr. Downey!" But of course, it was time to go.

Beth, frantic, came running outside to find her. The doctor braced herself.

"You left your new business cards!"

Graciously, she handed the box of cards to Downey.

"My gosh, Beth! Thank you so much," said the doctor.

"Good luck," said Beth. "It's been terrific working with you!" And she turned and went back inside.

Dr. Downey waited a moment, threw the business cards into the nearby trash can, got into her car, and drove off into the night.

Telescoping

A simple suburban living room.   MARK ATLAS, a young adult, sits on a couch, smiling absently, bored. While he sits perfectly still, around him – people, the world, life – whizz by at a fantastic speed.

BOOMING NARRATOR: Mark Atlas – genius communications major – is actually a mutant able to slow his metabolism whenever he gets bored! When Mark gets extremely bored he can travel great distances! To the future! *Mark Atlas – Telescoping!*

Mark still sits on the couch, smiling his empty blank stare, his eyes half-shut. BETSY – young adult, old-fashioned, cute, blonde, plump – sits next to him. SOUND rises of her talking to him, trying to get his attention.

BETSY: Mark –!? Mark!!

She shakes him. He comes to life.

MARK: What –? Where? Betsy –!

BETSY: You were telescoping again!

MARK: Sorry, honey. It's just – I'm a genius, see – and sometimes –

BETSY: You can't scope-out, tonight, Mark! If we're going to get married, you've got to make a good impression on my father!

MARK: I will, Betsy! I promise! I love you!

Betsy relaxes.

BETSY: Oh, Mark. That's what's important! Our love for each could never be boring! You know I feel so –

Mark spaces out again. Betsy shakes him.

BETSY: Mark –!

MARK: What –! Who –?!

DAD (*OS*): Ready in there?

MARK: Honey, let's get out of here! It's so dull! Let's telescope!

BETSY: Mark, I can't telescope. No one can tele-scope, but you. The rest of us can only try to catch up with you later.

MARK: Such a shame.

DAD, elderly and slow-moving, comes in with a big, roasted turkey.

DAD: Take a look at that bird! Don't get a turkey bigger'n that out of the country!

MARK: It's sure a big bird, sir!

Dad starts to carve the turkey. Betsy pours drinks for everyone.

BETSY: Looks wonderful, Dad!

DAD: Well, Mark, now Betsy tells me you're a genius!

MARK: That's right, sir.

DAD: Bit of an inventor, myself! I guess you're familiar with the typewriter lever?

BETSY: Oh, Dad – Mark doesn't want to hear about your –

DAD: Now, Betsy – he's a genius! It's shop talk to him! Now Mark, when I was a boy we had an old typewriter. And it was old. Old as the Ceder Oak that leans near the thresher. Old as the dew on the fresh mornin' grass. Old as the Baler scars – up and down my arm...

Betsy and her Dad freeze. We HEAR Mark's thoughts.

MARK: Wow, this conversation's tough. Maybe I'll just telescope to the end of the evening

Suddenly Dad's VOICE speeds up at an alarming rate. Mark remains bored, smiling, nodding his head.

MARK: Uh huh, uh huh...

There are blinding flashes of light and color as time flies by in seconds. The lights dim. When they come back up, Mark sits alone at the table. In the place of Betsy, Dad and the turkey are skeletons. There are cobwebs everywhere, and the tablecloth has rotted away.

TWO MEN, wearing beat-up, yellow, radiation suits, rush on. They fire laser weapons off-stage.

MAN 1: Rat bastard!

MAN 2: Die, Furgrabber!

MAN 1: Hurry! Back away! Others are coming!

MAN 1 barricades the door. MAN 2 pulls out a Geiger counter and checks the room. He looks at the skeletons and then notices Mark.

MARK: Uh huh, uh huh, uh huh...

MAN 2: Brownnose – look! He's alive!

Man 2 pokes Mark. Mark turns his head, regaining consciousness, and looks at Man 2.

MARK: Hello! When am I?

MAN 1: You're "way in the future." The year 2056.

MARK: Whoa! Big one! (*looking at skeletons*) Aw – poor Betsy.

He stands proudly and offers his hand.

MARK: Mark Atlas – Telescoping!

MAN 1: I'm Brownnose and this is Cheepdate. We're of the resistance.

MARK: Wow! You have exciting names! Did I miss anything?

Man 1 and 2 look at each other, shocked.

MAN 2: Only nuclear holocaust!

MARK: Well, that must've been very exciting!

MAN 2: It was horrific!

MAN 1 (*considering*): Horrific...but exciting!

MARK: How exciting!

MAN 1: Say – if you're a time-traveler, you could help us –

MAN 2: You could go back to the past and stop World War III! Stop the rodent people from taking over!

MAN 1: Stop President Trump from pushing the button in the first place!

MARK: Whoa! Guys! I'm sorry, but I can only time-travel when I'm bored!

MAN 1 and 2 look at each other.

MAN 1 (*to Man 2*): Tell him about your trip to Cape Hatteras.

MARK: No, wait! I kind of like it here!

MAN 2 (*droning*): Well, we didn't get started right away – I didn't want to drive to the Cape – but Maggie thought it would be less expensive than flying. Also, she gets this stomach thing –

Suddenly, the RODENT PEOPLE burst through the door, gunning down Man 1 and 2. They grab Mark, shove him against a wall and hold guns to his head. The HEAD RODENT saunters around.

RODENT FLUNKIE: Sir! He's not like the others!

HEAD RODENT: Kill him.

MARK: Wait! Wait! One last request –!

The Rodents freeze. We hear Mark's thoughts.

MARK: I'll trick them into boring me –

HEAD RODENT: Yeah, I heard that. Kill him!

Suddenly, RYAN GOSLING bursts into the room, laconically gunning down the Rodent People.

RYAN: Uhm. I'm almost certain there won't be any more killing today.

MARK: RYAN GOSLING!

Ryan sits down in front of the still captive Mark and begins droning on. Mark watches him.

RYAN: Y'know, Mark…it's interesting I've survived far enough into the future…to save you. It reminds me of an action picture I worked on in Los Angeles. Some might call it an action picture…others might call it a thriller. Still others might call it…an action-thriller…with dancing. Anyway, that's not important right now…

MARK: Uh huh, uh huh, uh huh –

Ryan's VOICE speeds up. LIGHTS whiz, flash, and go out. When they come back up, Mark is sitting near Betsy and her Dad again, at the moment he left.

DAD: …seemed obvious to me what the thing needed was a lever to advance the roller. I started tinkering, as I said, and I got this thing worked up with really just a kitchen fork...

MARK: Uh huh, uh huh, uh huh...

Dad starts speeding up, again.

NARRATOR: Will Mark be able to stop World War III? Or will he scope out? Tune in next week for another occasionally diverting episode of: *Mark Atlas: Telescoping!*

Hamlet (Epilogue)

A ghostly Danish moor. Fog rolls and lifts. HAMLET, depressed, and with a large bloody wound, wanders about.

HAMLET: Dad?! Dad!

The KING, an old, voluminous ghost in white sheets, enters dramatically.

KING: HAAAAAAAM – LET! HAAAAA –

HAMLET: Yeah. Hey – over here.

KING: Hamlet! Avenge me! Avenge –

HAMLET: Right. Did that.

Hamlet gestures to the bloody, gaping wound on his side.

KING: Oh. Oh! Wow! Ouch!

HAMLET: Yup.

KING: So – so – how'd that go then?

Slowly, and horrifically, the entire cast of HAMLET lurches onto the stage, moaning, wounded, poisoned, and writhing. LAERTES, POLONIUS, and

CLAUDIUS all have bleeding stab wounds. GERTRUDE is green and covered in wine. OPHELIA is green and covered in seaweed, her clothing blotched and ripped. Various OTHERS with wounds, carrying skulls, come in. The King watches them, amazed.

HAMLET: Not so well, actually.

KING: Holy mackerel! *Everybody?*

HAMLET: Pretty much.

KING: Boy! When you avenge, *you avenge!*

HAMLET: Yeah. Got a little crazy.

The crowd, pathetic and unguided, wanders over to the King. He addresses them.

KING: So…who's up for poker?

BLACKOUT

Across the Tundra

December 22, 1969.
Just turn around
was the scratched record endlessly repeating in my head.
This is stupid. I'm stupid.
I should just turn around.
But when I got to Dell Farms, and it was farther back than forward, my dogged, irrational *Want* kept me moving straight on ahead.

The lukewarm water was taking way too long to heat up the thermometer. And then I noticed Dad's cigarettes and lighter on the back of the toilet. So, I flicked his Bic and held the flame under the thermometer bulb, and with a quick, tiny *POP* it exploded shattering glass and mercury everywhere. My heart beating furiously, I quickly unrolled sheets and sheets of toilet paper and sopped up (or at least contained) the glass and liquid metal, and flushed the whole thing down the toilet, praying it wouldn't clog. It didn't. And I found and opened a new thermometer and ran it under the now warmer water.
101°.
Perfect.

"You get too excited over the holidays, Em," my mother said. "You make yourself sick."
"I know. I know," I said. "I'm sorry."

"I won't have time to come see you at lunch. Not with this storm."

Dad poked his head in. "Why don't you take her to the doctor?"

"She's got a low fever. She doesn't need a doctor."

"I'll be okay. I can make myself soup."

"Dee'll be home by three. I'll be home by 5:30. You'll survive till then."

Dee poked her head in. "Faker. She's totally faking!"

I hated Dee.

"Could you close the door?" I moaned. "It's drafty."

"Maybe I should stay and watch after her?" said Dee.

"You get to school," Mom barked.

The wind was brutal despite every inch of my body being heavily covered, head to toe. Goddamn snow from the past three days had piled up, and by 9:30 a.m. it had started to come down again in thick, globby clouds.

The first leg up Donner Road, a tree-lined, closely pocketed residential street, was all steep uphill and I stayed on the sidewalks as there was nowhere else to go. If a car came by I'd have to crouch down or hide behind a tree. I couldn't move fast in the dense snow and my thick boots, so running was not an option. And if someone stopped me I had no clever excuse for what I was doing. So, I had to be sure that no one stopped me.

I thought I could make the trip in about four hours. Two up, two back, give or take. I'd never actually walked it all before, and certainly not during a snowstorm. But I was pretty sure I could be back by lunchtime, which was way before Dee would get home.

Fortunately, there was no traffic on Donner. I went slow, blending in to the bleak, ubiquitous snowdrifts and feeling invisible, something that I was used to. I imagined that hidden out here in the pure white, I would've made an excellent spy.

Want drove me up the hill. And *Want* had me slogging in knee deep drifts. But I was pretty sure what I wanted was still at the mall.

covet covet covet

No! It's an Adventure! I told myself. It wasn't crazy. And so, what if it was crazy? It wasn't a crime. I wasn't hurting anyone. It was a fair trade. A better-than-fair trade!

I reached the top of the hill and shuffled two blocks out of my way to Rose Briar to avoid the elementary school that sat atop Donner. To go around would take an extra ten minutes, but I couldn't take a chance on any kids or teachers spotting me, a wandering truant.

Goddamn snow. Tobogganing and sledding and snowball fights. Forget it. It was too goddamn cold with your face freezing and your nostrils getting all stiff and inverted. I had already spent three days shoveling and it was still coming down. But you couldn't not shovel. Not since Dad decided you were old enough. And six-year-old idiot Jay watching from inside the house only made it worse.

"I wanna shovel!" He'd say. "Why can't I shovel?"

"He can do my shoveling," I'd offer.

"You stay out of it!" Mom would say.

The Kapweskies got extra allowance for shoveling. And with this much goddamn snow they were probably rich by now. But we didn't get any allowance to begin with.

"It's slave labor!" I'd say.

"Damn right it is," Dad would say. "Now, shut up and shovel."

I circled back over Riley and made time towards Katie Marshall's house. Snow had gotten in my boots. My socks were damp, and my face was tight with windburn. And I wasn't halfway to the mall yet. *I'm getting frostbite* I thought. *I'm losing toes*. But I couldn't go back. It was too late for that.

Around Katie's house – over the fence – and there was my first landmark, Dell Farms. Dell Farms' field was a pure white wasteland several acres across and straight through to the final part of my trip, Highway 25.

Balalaika strains from *Lara's Theme* (*Dr. Zhivago*) bounced through my head as I inched through the field. But even in Siberia I bet they couldn't have been as cold as I was. My back ached from hauling the heavy backpack – which I had to bring. And I did bring it, so it was good. I was covered.

covet covet covered.

My mind wandered. I wondered if any store in the mall sold a rope ladder. A rope ladder, I thought, could be a great, highly useful gift for pretty much anyone. It had a million uses, like you could unroll it out of your bedroom window during a fire, or you could just use it whenever you wanted to escape from somewhere high.

Then it occurred to me that if I got sick with fever it would actually serve me right, since I was supposed to be home with a fever anyway. And somehow that gave me comfort. But of course, I had to actually get back home first.

I gave a tractor chugging along in the far distance of the field a wide berth, and picked up my pace. My Goofy watch told me I'd walked 50 minutes already, but now I knew the mall was close.

Across the field, back on the sidewalk, two blocks over and I was on Highway 25, a busy road with traffic. My invisibility was gone now, and I had to move super quickly. I kept my head focused forward. No eye contact with drivers. Didn't want anyone to glance over or stop. *Keep moving. Keep moving.* Past the bowling alley, the drive-through liquor, the McDonald's.

Mom and I had stopped at the McDonald's on the way to the mall two days earlier as a treat. I loved McDonald's and would've lived there if I could've. And Mom told me maybe next March we might even have my birthday there.

We ate, and as we returned to the car, she steered me from a bag lady, who was leaning up against a brown, beaten-up station wagon and staring at the ground. Mom offered her a quarter and the rest of her McDonald's coffee, both of which the woman took, nodding appreciatively. As we hurried past the wagon, I could swear I saw two young kids – a boy and girl maybe – inside the car, and that they stared back out at me.

Achy and exhausted, I staggered past McDonald's, past the medical building, the Italian and Greek restaurants. And finally, there it was: Brightstown Mall.

Brightstown Mall, an outdoor mall, was a ghost town of linked stores that few people shopped at since glamorous Tri-County had opened two years ago. I hurried to the center area where all the open lanes of stores converged and the "You Are Here" map was located. And what I'd come all this way for was still there: the Christmas donation bin – a huge, green and white cardboard bin stuffed with dolls, toys, games, and boxes. On top was a large sign that said "Give to the Poor. Only Three More Days." And the bin was even more jam-packed than when I'd seen it two days ago with my mother.

I opened my backpack and took out the large, awful, plastic ring puzzle that I knew some other kid would no doubt enjoy much more than I would. And I put it into the bin and removed the only thing – the *only* thing – that I'd been thinking of for the past 24 hours:

A perfect, pink, utterly beautiful *I Dream of Jeannie* lunchbox.

And it was truly perfect, better even than I imagined it would be. It didn't just look good, it *felt* good, felt *right* with me, like it *belonged with me.* And I gingerly shoved it into my backpack. And as I turned to leave, a nearby elderly shopper sneezed.

"Bless you," I said.

"Thank you," she said, and went back to her shopping.

And I ran towards the highway.

I Dream of Jeannie was simply the best show on television. Jeannie was magical and beautiful, and everyone loved her, and she could do absolutely anything. One Saturday night, when my folks were having a card game, I dressed only in a towel and every time someone in the house needed something, I'd bow and say *Yes, Master. Yes, Master.*

"Hey, Em! Go grab me a beer!"

Yes, Master!

Dad and his friends thought I was hysterical. Mom thought differently.

"Stop that!" she'd yell. "Go put some clothes on!"

I was back home and in my pajamas in less than an hour. I blew dry my clothes, shoes, hat, coat, and scarf till they were spotless and warm. I still had all my toes and no fever, and I made myself some soup. And since I had a couple hours before Dee would get home, I spent the rest of the afternoon lazing around in bed, appreciating the perfection of my new lunchbox, and happily, sleepily reading TV Guide.

I didn't know it at the time, but decades later I'd discover that I – a slightly pudgy, 10-year-old girl with poorly cut bangs – had just slogged through 6.4 miles of suburban tundra.

For a lunchbox.

By the next morning I knew I had to get rid of the lunchbox.

Lumbering through the snow I had fantasized that I would take my new lunchbox to school and everyone would smile and be jealous and want to eat lunch with me every day. And it would be so cool, and we would all talk about *I Dream of Jeannie* and *Bewitched* – which was good but not nearly as good as *Jeannie* – and *Laugh In* which was pretty good and also real funny. But of course, now I realized that I could never ever use the lunchbox, could never even take it out of its hiding place in the hat box under my bed. Because if I did any of that, well then, my mother would know.

Where did you get that? she'd ask. *Who gave it to you?*

She wouldn't rest till she'd found out and I couldn't lie to her. She'd see right through me.

I could never use the lunchbox.

I was so angry with myself. So enraged. This beautiful pink thing with big eyes and dancing cartoon Jeannie's all over it – and I couldn't even show it to anyone! How could I have not thought of that!? It was so obvious!

And now more than ever, I kept hearing Father Craig's voice in my head. *Covet covet covet.*

He had done his pre-Christmas sermon last Sunday with a special message to kids about not coveting and being happy with what you had. *Dare not to covet* he stated over and over. *Temper thy covetous thoughts. Remember, as you congregate, that to covet is a top ten Sin.* Father Craig must've said *covet* 54 times in that sermon. He said *covet* so much the word started to lose its meaning for me.

He'd say *covet* and I'd imagine sitting on the living room couch with my feet up on the *covet*. Mmm, nice plush *covet*. Relaxing!

But oh man I had *coveted*. How I had *coveted!*

Part of the problem was that I had known exactly what I was getting for Christmas this year. Last year, Dee showed me where Mom and Dad had hidden our presents – under the tarp in the far back of the garage loft. I had been mad at Dee for telling me. But this year I looked on my own, and the shock that went through me was heavy. The pile was much smaller than last year's, and the gifts and toys were *awful*. There were knock-off toys, toys that looked used and re-taped, and the best of the lot was a *Dude Ranch Barbie* that I had pleaded for – but never gotten – the previous Christmas, and had since lost all interest in. (It was, after all, *last year's* cool toy.) The newest and nicest thing marked for me this year was some giant, plastic, purple ring puzzle that no normal boy or girl would ever want.

"This can't be all of it. There has to be more coming, right?"

"Of course, that's it," said Dee. "They cut back Dad's hours. That's as good as it gets."

"But why are they having a party if –"

"They're not gonna *not* have their party – it's the biggest thing they do all year!"

Tears welled-up in my eyes.

"Are we out of money?"

"Jesus!" said Dee. "It's just temporary! Everything's fine!"

I couldn't sleep. The lunchbox was a *Tell-Tale Heart* beating maniacally under my bed and burning a hole straight up through the mattress. Sooner or later Mom would clean under there and then the Gates of All Hell would open.

What have you done!?

But what could I do? Throwing away a perfectly good lunchbox would not just be wasteful, but horrifically uncharitable. And besides, it wasn't the lunchbox's fault it was trapped under my bed. It was *my* fault. I had taken its purpose away!

The bin had said "Three More Days" and that was two days ago. Time was running out. I couldn't fake getting sick again and I certainly couldn't ask Mom to take me back to the mall. I needed a plan.

"Just throw it out!" said Dee. "What are you – five years old?! No one wants to hear about your stupid lunchbox!"

I had decided to confide in Dee only because I had run out of options. Besides, she was 16 and, theoretically, might have ideas. But in fact, she was completely, utterly useless.

"Grow up, Em! Some people have real problems!"

I went back to my room and slammed the door. Dee slammed her own door and locked it.

"*No slamming doors!*" Mom screamed from downstairs.

Dee's big thing now was locking herself in her room and seething over the latest boy who had dumped her. Jay and I weren't allowed to lock our doors. But Dee said that, at 16, if Mom and Dad didn't let her lock her door she'd move the hell out and live downtown in a hotel. She acted like she meant it, but I sincerely doubted she had the balls.

I buried my face in my pillow and cried. Dee barged in.

"You are *so* unbelievably stupid!" she said.

"Go away!" I said. "I'm sorry I even told you!"

"What I should do," she said, "is go down and tell her exactly what you did!"

"You wouldn't!"

"But if you calm down and behave yourself," she said, "I'll help you."

I gulped for air, unable to stop crying.

"*What's going on up there?!*" Mom yelled.

"Nothing!" said Dee, looking at me, angrily.

"Admit that this is stupid, and I'll help you," she said.

"It's – it's – it's – it's – it's not – it's –" I couldn't catch my breath.

She glared at me.

"It's stupid," I said.

Suddenly, I could breathe again.

"You really can't throw it away?" she asked.

"No. No – it's –"

"You put another toy in there, so you didn't completely steal it –"

"It was a trade!"

"Sort of."

"It was!"

"Okay."

Wow. For once, we agreed on something.

"Can't you just donate it somewhere else?"

"I think I should put it back where I found it," I said. "I think that's what I should do."

"But it doesn't –"

"I've thought about this," I said. "A lot."

"I see that."

"What if the person who donated it the first time came back and noticed it was gone? And called the police?"

She stared at me, confused.

"Are you out of your mind?"

"It could happen!"

"It could not happen! At all! *Ever!*"

"You don't know that!"

"No one cares about your stupid –"

"I want you both down here now!" Mom screeched. "We have guests arriving!"

I got out my backpack and began digging under the bed.

"I'm taking it back," I said. "Right now."

I was halfway down the stairs. Dee trailed me, pulling her coat on. Mom stared at us, aghast.

"Where do you think you're going?"

"Left my coat at Katie's," I said.

"Which coat?"

"The other one."

She looked at Dee.

"You want her walking around alone in the dark, with all the drunks out?" said Dee.

"Five minutes," said Mom. "No more!"

"I can do this by myself!" I bellowed, trudging back up Donner. "I don't need you to come with me! I don't even care who knows! I don't care at all anymore! Send me to jail! Tell everyone! I don't care!"

Dee shoved me down on the snow-covered sidewalk and knelt down hard on my chest.

"Get off!" I yelled, struggling.

"If I get off will you listen?!"

"No – yes – fine!"

She let me up and took the lead, walking with a determined look in her eye.

"Where are you going?" I called.

Three blocks up, she stopped at a brown, icicle-covered Tudor and rang the bell. A slouching teenage boy with sandy hair and a crap t-shirt on answered the door. He looked at Dee, annoyed.

"What?" he said.

"We need a ride, Mike."

"Forget it," he said, shutting the door on her. But Dee jammed her foot in the crack, forcing it open. The boy fell back, surprised, pissed.

"Hey – hey!" he yelled. "What the –"

"Your parents here?" asked Dee.

"Why?"

She looked at him, seriously, then leaned over and whispered something in his ear. He froze and became completely pale.

"*What?*" he said.

Dee stepped back and glared at him.

"We need a ride, Mike. Now. *Right now.* Can you handle that?"

Mike's dad stepped near the door, curious.

"Mike?" he said. "All okay?"

"Yeah. Yeah," he said, grabbing his jacket and keys and shoving Dee outside. Dee glanced over at me, her eyes lit up. A minute later we were in Mike's car, heading towards the highway.

"This is the definition of uncool, Dee," said Mike.

"No one asked you," she said.

"So, what – are you kidding?" he mumbled to her. "Because if you're trying to be funny, you're not being funny. At all."

"What's the difference," she said. "Why should you care?"

He stewed, and glanced over at her.

"I'm supposed to be home tonight!" he said. "We're having people over."

"So are we, shithead. So, the sooner you get us there and back the better."

I sat in the back seat, gripping my backpack. Dee stared coolly out the window. Mike kept glancing over at her, trying to read her anger.

"Mike!" I called from the back. "Do you have a rope ladder?"

"What? No."

"What if you needed one?"

"Why would I need one in a car?"

"What if you, like, drove off a cliff or a bridge and you were halfway off, and you needed a rope ladder to climb down to a tree limb or something?"

"Then I guess I would die."

"Not if you had a rope ladder," I said, confidently.

And Dee and Mike briefly looked at each other.

Brightstown Mall. Mike pulled up near the curb. I got out.

"Goes much faster when someone drives you!" I said, cheerfully. I thought this was a great joke, but no one laughed. I could be on *Laugh In*.

"Do whatever you're doing and let's go," Mike snapped.

I turned, slipped on a patch of ice, went flying feet up, and landed hard on my back.

"Em!" Dee yelled. "You okay?"

Bruised but unhurt, I pulled off the backpack and opened it. I looked inside.

"*NO!*" I yelled. "*No no no no!!!*"

Mike and Dee looked out their windows. I held up the lunchbox. The side with the big pink eyes was entirely caved in.

The three of us entered Oberts – the large mall pharmacy – just as the tall, lanky clerk was closing up.

"We need a lunchbox *stat*!" I said. This was something doctors said on *Medical Center*.

The clerk shuffled through the tins on the back shelf, holding up different ones, moving others aside.

"This one?" he asked, holding a lovely new *Bonanza* box.

"No! No, the pink one!" I said, pointing.

"Ah," he said, handing me the lunchbox. "Well, that's very pretty for you."

"It's not for me. It's for charity," I said.

"Well, that's swell," he said. "That's $2.50, please."

Dee and Mike looked at me. I looked back at them. Dee and Mike looked at each other and then me, again. The clerk looked at all three of us, confused.

"*Thieves! Gypsies! Degenerates!*" the clerk yelled from the door of Oberts. He went back inside and picked up the store telephone.

We bolted down the mall lane, with me clutching at the new lunchbox for dear life.

"Okay, so *now* you've stolen!" yelled Dee.

"I thought we were coming to donate," I yelled. "I didn't bring any money!"

"I had nothing to do with this!" yelled Mike. "I am *not* going to jail!"

"Aiding and abetting!" yelled Dee.

"It's not stealing!" I yelled. "I have $2.50 at home! We'll bring it later!"

"We'll be in prison, later!" yelled Dee.

We got to the center of the mall, where all the stores converged, and stopped cold.

"Where's the bin?" said Mike.

We looked around. The entire center area was empty except for dilapidated green benches and untended plants. The bin was gone.

"It was here," I said.

"Hey! Hey, you!" yelled the Oberts clerk running towards us with a grizzled Mall Security Guard trotting alongside him.

"Come on," said Dee. We ran to the parking lot. A minute later we were back on the highway with two hot lunchboxes.

Highway 25.

"That's it," said Mike. "I'm taking you home."

"We have to get rid of these lunchboxes," said Dee.

"Wait – I know," said Mike. "Here –"

He reached back, grabbed the dented one and flung it out of his open window. Behind us, there was a *screech*, and the sounds of a car swerving, and metal being crushed. My eyes bugged out.

"*What the hell, Mike!?*" said Dee.

"Gimme the other one," said Mike.

"No!" I said, holding it tight, and then, "*Wait! Wait! Pull over!*"

Mike lurched the car and suddenly we were in the McDonald's parking lot.

"There! Pull over next to that station wagon there. The brown one," I said.

Mike pulled next to the battered wagon that I'd seen two days ago with Mom. The old woman was still there giving McDonald's scraps to the two kids in the car. I could see now the little girl was about Jay's age. I got out of Mike's car and went to them. The woman eyed me, confused.

"Hello. Hi. Merry Christmas," I said. "I'm sorry to bother you. I just –"

The girl looked at me, a little frightened.

"Hey, how are you?" I said. "Would you – would you maybe, like a new lunchbox?"

I held it out to her. She eyed it, curious, but excited.

"It's brand new. Really. You can have it. It's all yours. I mean it. No strings attached."

The girl looked at the woman. The woman looked at me, slowly, then approvingly, at the girl. I handed her the lunchbox and her eyes lit up like magic. Then Mike was next to me, practically towering over me, and reaching out to the little boy in the car.

"I don't have anything nice – but I got this," he said, handing a stained, beat-up NY Giants cap to the boy. The woman rolled her eyes, but nodded to the boy, who took the gift, eagerly. Mike looked at me and shrugged.

"Merry Christmas!" I said, and we got back in the car and sped off.

As we drove, Mike looked at me in the rearview mirror.

"Yer a lunatic," he said

And I smiled, content.

Two days earlier I had been to Oberts with my mother. I loved Oberts – the mall drugstore with its candy and comic books and not-so-bad drugstore toys. But the best part was the massive number of new lunchboxes lined up on the shelves behind the counter.

"Pick one you like," my Mom had said to me. And my heart beat so fast, because now I knew – *I knew* – there was another Christmas gift coming this year that wasn't in the garage. And I knew exactly which lunchbox I wanted.

I pointed to the pink one, and the nice, tall clerk handed it to me. And Mom smiled and paid him.

And then, silently, she led me to the center of the mall where we could donate our most prized earthly possessions to those more in need.

"Put it in, Em! We don't have time for this!"

"No!" I said, clinging tightly to the box. "No, it's mine! This is mine! I thought we were donating something else!"

"*Don't be stupid!*" she said, tearing the lunchbox away from me and throwing it in. And I stared, horrified, as my perfect new lunchbox fell sideways into the donations bin. And squeezing my arm, she dragged me, screaming and crying, back to the car.

By the time Mike pulled up to our house – more than an hour and a half since when we'd left – it was dark out. The house glowed and bustled with holiday lights, and family and guests making merry.

"Thank you, Mike," I said and got out and started towards the house. Dee, still in the car, hesitated.

"Why don't you come in?" she asked Mike.

He looked down.

"Dad'll be worried," he said.

"Yeah," she said. "Well, whatever, anyway. Thanks." And she got out of the car.

"Dee," he said.

She looked back at him.

"I'll call you," he said.

And at the door, Mom, in apron, stood waiting for us, arms crossed, her face beet red.

Later that night, I found Dee in the corner of the living room, among a sea of family. She had melted into my father's recliner and looked sleepy, but content. I sat cross-legged on the floor next to her. And for a long while we both sat and said nothing. Finally, I broke the silence.

"I think that was pretty cool," I said. "I think."

"It was *awesome*," she said.

"Dee," I said. "What did you whisper to Mike?"

She looked at me with a long, wistful glance but said nothing. She just took a deep breath and gave a half-smile. Whatever she said or didn't say didn't matter anymore. And after that night, we never mentioned it again.

Christmas morning brought a stack of neatly wrapped presents under our massive tree. Jay, tearing open gifts, was as cheery and thrilled and surprised as ever. And Dee and I faked our surprise as effectively as we always had. In fact, every time we gasped or squealed, we looked at each other, happy and knowingly.

And then my mother stepped over to me with a final box that was new. A lunchbox-sized present that I hadn't seen or accounted for. And she smiled as she gave it to me, as if she knew more about the last few days than she'd let on. I took the box and tore it open, and there, on the inside, was a brilliant new Polaroid camera. And a package of film. And a 10 flash-bulb stick.

Oh my God!!!!! I thought. *A Polaroid camera! No one at school had a Polaroid camera!*

I hugged my mother tightly. And then I spent the rest of the day taking instant snapshots of her and Dad and Jay and everyone in the house, and the house itself, and the cars, and the neighbors, and the neighbors' cars, and the dog. And we went over to Mike's and took a picture of Mike. And Mike and Dee – and that was a little weird but nice. And then I ran out of film.

So, the very next day we went to Oberts and bought more film. And Dee took a great picture of me giving the very nice clerk at Oberts the two dollars and fifty cents I owed him, which was almost – but not quite – all the money I had in the world. Which was fine.

Because, honestly, I didn't even miss the stupid lunchbox.

Somewhere Other than Earth

SPACE. A tiny, 1950's-era, Buster Crabbe-type rocket vaults through the cosmos.

BOOMING NARRATOR: Fleeing from an Earth overrun by personal fitness trainers, Mark Savage and his pal, Dani, wander the stars in their two-person rocket, Charlemagne! Their destination: *Somewhere Other Than Earth!*

A DENSE JUNGLE. MARK and DANI – in space outfits – make their way through a clearing. Suddenly, they're ambushed by four ferocious monsters: GORGO, RODAN, MOTHRA and KONG.

RODAN: Humans!!!

MARK: We come in peace!

The monsters circle them, warily.

DANI: Is this the Planet of Agnostic Amazons?

MARK: Is it the Planet of Living Chia Pcts?

KONG: No! This is the Planet Where Everyone's a Yoga Instructor!

The monsters start doing weird stretches and stances.

MONSTERS: Stretch with me! No, me! Over here! Om! Ommm!

DANI: But we just left a planet like that!

RODAN (*doing Crow pose*): Look! I can do Crow pose! Caw! Caw!

MOTHRA (*standing like a tree*): I am a tree! Would you like an apple?!

GORGO: I have many yoga mats at home!! ARRGH!

Mark whips out his ray-gun.

MARK: Alright! That's enough! Get back!

Dani sees something on the ground. She points, frightened.

DANI: Mark! Tiny intelligent bugs in yoga pants! The kind you can wear on an airplane without getting arrested!

The Monsters stomp on the bugs, aggressively.

MARK: Stop! Stop! Oh God! Are you *all* so desperately enlightened!?

MOTHRA: Sometimes – I can't stretch all the way down –

RODAN: I – I often eat at Taco Bell!

Kong thumps his chest.

KONG: And where are *your* yoga mats?!

MARK: We left them on Earth! We're trying to get away from all that!

The monsters move towards them, ferociously.

DANI: Wait! Look at this!

Dani quickly gets into downward dog pose. The Monsters gasp, stunned.

MONSTERS: Downward dog!!!

MOTHRA: And done…to perfection!

The monsters fall to the ground, humbling themselves.

RODAN: Forgive us!

GORGO: We were rude!

KONG: Teach me how to breathe correctly!

OTHERS: No, me! Me!

The enraged monsters begin battling amongst themselves.

MARK (*to Dani*): Come on!

They run off. Everyone freezes.

BOOMING NARRATOR: Where will Mark and Dani find themselves next?! *Somewhere Other Than Earth!*

The Bone Nest

Farel, the eight-year-old wolfboy, squat upon the banquet table unceremoniously devouring what was left of a large pheasant, much to the Queen's distress. The Grand Hall was an utter mess: chairs and tables were overturned, the buffet had been routed, and all decorations lay mangled. The Queen's horrified guests had left hours ago, and now she stood, fists clenched, staring violently at Farel.

"He should be with the dogs!" she snapped. "I've half a mind to put him there myself!"

"Darling," started the King, trying to keep a calm demeanor. "We need to be patient. We must give him time."

Zanon – the boy's elderly instructor – hid behind the King and watched them, trembling fearfully.

"We've given him time!" she wailed. "He's ruined three parties! I've hardly *any* friends left!"

"We need to give more," said the King.

"Why?!"

"You know very well why," he said. "Because he is family."

"*Your* family. Not mine," she said. "He barely acts human!"

The King's brow furrowed.

"Hold your tongue!" he snapped. "The boy is blood – and while he remains so, he will be treated as such!"

Farel ate quietly, regarding the bickering couple with bored curiosity. Zanon stared at the boy, pleading with his eyes for some sort of recognition. But Farel simply chewed and uttered a quiet, high-pitched yowl.

"*I* am blood," said the Queen, jutting her prominent nose at the King. "And I'll be damned if I let this animal ruin one more of my gatherings."

"This is on *you*," she shrieked savagely at Zanon. "You're the one charged with making him *presentable!*"

"I – I have tried," stammered Zanon. "For – for months!"

"Well now, you have *days*," she said. "If he's not *fixed* within three days he goes to the dogs! And you? You go to feed them!"

She stormed out of the hallway. Zanon wobbled, gasping for breath. The King looked at him, sternly.

"Get hold of yourself," said the King.

"Y-yes, sire," bowed Zanon, weakly.

The King approached Farel, and leaned down to look at him. Farel turned shyly away.

"He's so much like my brother," said the King. "He has his eyes. But his inability to embrace even a smattering of our customs, our language, makes no sense. He is royal blood! I don't care that my brother married – a lupine – or whatever her people were. I met them! You met them! They spoke the language of the kingdom!"

"They did, your highness."

The King reached out, helplessly, to the old instructor.

"Then why can't I reach him?"

"I've – I've employed all my skills, sire –"

"And what haven't you tried?!" he asked, knowing full well what the answer was.

Zanon hesitated and then finally said what they'd both been thinking.

"Magic."

The ascent to the aerie was treacherous and Farel and Zanon had already seen their entire three-man consort fall to their deaths. They'd been climbing since dawn and had braved terrible winds. Farel was not a natural climber, while Zanon was grossly weighed down by the enormous pack on his back. But finally, they'd reached the summit, *the Bone Nest*.

The Bone Nest was the home of the creature known as the Demon Roc. The nest itself was an enormous structure built entirely of jagged, bleached white bones. The bones were human, elven, animal, animal hybrid, trollish and so on. The Demon Roc was not particular about what breed or nation filled its nest, and its home was sacred ground.

The origins of the Roc were that of myth. A popular version was that eons ago the creature had once been a wizard or witch, but had transformed itself to fight a great war that had ended poorly for the Roc, leaving it eternally frozen in the form of the monster bird. Now, it regularly soared the countryside terrorizing villages, and capturing travelers and treasures to decorate its nest. Any adventurer mad enough to trespass the nest, would suffer a quick and horrific demise.

The bones that were the aerie walls climbed ten feet high to the nest's peak. Over time, the winds and rain had polished them to a glistening white. Farel and his instructor descended into its bowels, where Zanon was relieved to find the Roc absent.

The interior of the nest was putrid and filled with half-eaten forms piled upon one another and not yet picked clean. Hidden among the carnal wreckage was the bird's loot. Much was purely ornamental – torn cloths, lost shields and banners, gold-plated furniture – all nestled among thousands of coins and gems. And, in the far northeast corner of the nest, lay three colossal eggs.

While Farel gazed at the sky, feeling the fierce wind whip through his fur, Zanon dug furiously through the detritus, wondering if he'd even find the item he was looking for. And if he did find it, would he know what to do with it? His knowledge of magic was limited. What he did know was that they could take nothing with them, for to do so meant the bird could find them anywhere. Any object they found, they'd have to use there, in the nest, and they'd have precious little time to do much of anything.

Zanon found many things – weapons, jewels – and finally, what he'd come for: *items of power*. He found what must surely have been a *Serum of Transformation*. But would it improve Farel's appearance or make it worse? And if it improved his appearance, would he still retain his difficult, lupine nature? It was too great a risk. Zanon found a *Cloak of Snow* that might hide them. But it was cumbersome, and he knew it would only momentarily fool the bird. A *Transportation Compass* he uncovered was likely useful, but he couldn't quite grasp how to make it work. And then he found exactly what he was looking for: *The Crystal Horn*.

The Crystal Horn was an enchanted ram's horn formed from a single piece of translucent quartz. One needed only to blow it loudly and close enough, and the willing listener would instantly gain all knowledge and use of the horn-blower's native language.

Such a device had surely been in no other hands for decades -- perhaps centuries. And with it, Zanon realized, he could become the world's greatest translator. With this magnificent tool, he could acquire wealth, bring men of any nation together, even end wars. And then he caught sight of the forlorn, shivering wolf-boy, and wondered how he could ever contemplate ending wars, if he couldn't help even one little Lupine.

Anxiously, Zanon concealed the horn in his cloak and made his way over to Farel. The boy was hunched over the cracked remnant of a mirror – a *scrying* mirror it seemed – the kind that could produce images of other lands and events. In the mirror appeared the ravages of a recent war. Trees were burned and charred, woods demolished, fields decimated. A thick smoke filled the landscape and everywhere – as far as the eye could see – lay the bodies of dead wolf people.

"Home," Farel uttered in a low, pained, whispery growl. It was the first words of the King's language he'd spoken aloud.

Zanon leaned close.

"It's – it's all gone," said Zanon. "But – but with this – you'll have a wonderful new gift –"

He lifted the crystal horn close to Farel's ear. But the boy turned on him, suddenly.

"No!" snarled the boy with a ferociousness that knocked Zanon backwards. Zanon dropped the horn and watched it shatter instantly against a large, jutting bone. His eyes went wide with panic, and he reached uselessly for the shards.

"Oh no – oh no –" he wailed. "What have you done?!"

Farel had returned, morosely, to his mirror.

"Home," he repeated, sadly.

"There is no home, you misfit!" Zanon shouted, taking him by the shoulders. "Don't you understand?! We're all that's left for you! We are your home! And now –"

But his words were drowned by the deafening roar of murderous, gargantuan *wings*. The Demon Roc appeared suddenly in the sky and began to bear down on them.

"*Gods!*" gurgled Zanon.

His head darted, searching for any kind of usable cover. Farel, with naïve spunk, stood on tiny haunches, grit his fangs and growled at the ominous bird. Zanon grabbed Farel under one arm and lumbered across the nest, while the boy continued to mew and spit. A broken half-limb tripped Zanon, and he and Farel fell. Calcified fragments and spurs stabbed into Zanon's arms and legs, wounding him, and he lay crumpled and bleeding as the Roc plunged towards them. Farel, atop Zanon, barked and growled, and the bird swooped back into a high arc, and shrieked the shriek of a predator teasing its prey.

Zanon, lurching in pain, got to his feet, grabbed Farel, and carried him quickly to the farthest edge of the bony wall. The bird came down. With his remaining strength, Zanon removed the bulk that had been weighing down his pack – a large, fresh boar's carcass – and heaved it over the side of the nest. Overwhelmed by its unnatural instincts, the Roc dove after the carcass engulfing it in a single bite, then flapped its wings to regain altitude. But a strange thing happened. Instead of flying, the bird suddenly lost all strength, and with a look of terror, plummeted to the earth below.

Zanon watched, gasping. Farel looked at him, perplexed.

"And that's what a pig filled to the brim with shot will do to you!" said Zanon. "But Gods know whether or not he's finished, so we'd best get clear of here!"

They camped deep in the woods that night, miles from the aerie and half a day's walk back to the castle. They sat near a large fire, the boy quietly chewing on the remains of a hare. The old teacher stared into the fire, nursing his wounds and miserably contemplating the reaction of the King and Queen to their failure.

And then suddenly, he noticed the boy nuzzling up next to him, as if seeking warmth, comfort. He turned, and the boy looked deeply, solemnly into his eyes.

"Home?" said the boy, simply.

"It's gone," said Zanon. "I'm so sorry. I wish I could bring you back to them. But I can't."

"Home," said Farel again. And he butted gently against Zanon, and made the closest thing he could to a fanged smiled.

Zanon looked at him, and understood.

"I – learn," growled Farel, quietly, humbly.

And Zanon took him under his arm.

"Yes," he said, comfortingly. "Yes, you will."

And they fell asleep together, and slept peacefully in the warmth of the fire.

The Ewok Scale

A press conference at NASA. GENERAL DORN comes out and speaks to several REPORTERS.

DORN: Thanks for joining us at NASA. Today, we'd like to review our recent policy change. Previously, our primary mission was to determine whether or not alien life of any kind whatsoever exists elsewhere in the universe. (*beat*) As of today, however, we're making a subtle change to that policy. Going forward, we will only be seeking out safe, small, happy, friendly, non-threatening life-forms. (*beat*) No life forms that might burn the flesh off our bodies, or suck out our brains, or stomp all over our towns. Just cute, cuddly, friendly life forms. That's what we want. Questions?

Reporters raise their hands and shout out.

REPORTER 1: So, no giant space krakens that shoot death rays?

DORN: No. However, Krakens that can fit in your pocket and purr gently are fine. Yes?

REPORTER 2: What about lizard men – the size of skyscrapers – with giant icky tentacles on their faces?

DORN: No. Now, see – that's a great example of exactly what we're trying to avoid. Yes?

REPORTER 3: What about microscopic, non-sentient, amoebas?

DORN: Are they poisonous?

REPORTER 3: Yes.

DORN: No.

REPORTER 4: Skgg-yak fwa vo nog-yak gwabba?

DORN: I'm sorry, could you repeat that?

Reporter 4 bangs on something on his wrist, then speaks in a stilted drone.

REPORTER 4: Sorry. What – about – shape-shifters – with – no – intention – whatsoever – of – gz-gragah – (*bangs on wrist*) infiltrating – your – society?

The other reporters look oddly at Reporter 4.

DORN: Let's make this easy. Going forward, we will only use the Ewok Scale.

An EWOK comes out, and cheerfully waves its hands. The reporters gasp. Reporter 4 remains highly agitated, and backs away from the Ewok.

DORN: Cute. Cuddly. Short. That's what we want.

Dorn affectionately shoves the Ewok. The Ewok, annoyed, jumps up and down and waves its hands, but then lowers its head, and sulks, defeated.

DORN: Alright, I'll wrap up there. But please visit NasaWimps.gov for future updates. Thank you.

Dorn steps down. The Ewok and Reporter 4 face off against each other, and HISS and circle each other for domination. Dorn and the other reporters watch, confused.

The Sixth Sister

Saturday. 12:30 a.m.

Conrad was experiencing a perfect moment.

He sat on his hotel room bed staring at the complete – *yes, complete* – set of Oneida LaVigne Silverplate XI steak knives – known to collectors as *The Six Sisters*. They were the holy grail of steak knives, and believed responsible for countless historical crimes and acts of mayhem.

By the late 1800s, the small Oneida Community in upstate New York was known for two things: a manufacturing business that crafted the finest cutlery in America; and having been founded as a utopian society that practiced, among other things, "complex marriages" allowing all members of the society to engage in free sexual relations with any other consensual member of the community. Older men and women regularly indoctrinated youngsters into this way of life and dissenting behavior was promptly chastised.

One scandal arose when Charles Maypool, a young smith hard at work on the LaVigne Silverplate set, urged his love, Henrietta, to flee the enclave and start a family with him in the world outside. When news of this subversion reached the town leaders, Maypool was put in stocks, while Henrietta was quickly "wed" to four of the community elders.

Weeks later, Maypool was released. But instead of resuming his duties, he retrieved his six Silverplate knives, snuck up on the four elders while they slept and slashed their throats, each with a different knife. With the fifth knife, he slew Henrietta. Then – keeping only the sixth knife for himself – he fled deep into the woods of upstate New York, never to be heard from again.

By 1900, the Oneida Community had abandoned its utopian dreams. The five sister knives abandoned by Maypool were individually dispersed and traded from one curio dealer to another. In due time, the knives fell into a role of infamy with some of the century's most horrific crimes attributed to them. Somehow, the five sisters always found their way back to one another. But the sixth sister was never recovered. Collectors searched endlessly for her. Presidents clamored for her. Ripley wanted her for his personal trove. To complete the set was a treasure hunter's mecca, but she never turned up.

Conrad Margolies, a dogged but reclusive dealer in antiquities and American crime memorabilia, had finally come to possess all five sister knives as well as their worn chestnut container. When he started getting letters about a possible sixth knife, he was skeptical. But everything the old woman had written to him rang true – its history, its markings – things no one could know without having actually seen and experienced the knives themselves. So, Conrad made a hotel reservation, packed his car, and set out on the arduous 300-mile drive.

Saturday. 10:30 p.m. The bar of the Marquis Hotel.

Conrad needed a drink before meeting the woman. *Who was she? Did she really have the Sixth Sister?*

And what would she want for it? Thousands? Hundreds of thousands? Did she know its history? And had the knife had any effect on her?

He swallowed his bourbon, and was unsurprised to see rival collector McCoy, with that awful pomaded moustache, suddenly sitting next to him.

"This is it, isn't it, Connie?" said McCoy.

"Wouldn't know. I'm here for Billy the Kid's boots."

"Bullshit," said McCoy. "Listen, Connie – I know people. We can do this together."

Conrad threw $20 on the bar and walked away.

"Don't hold out on me!" yelled McCoy. "*I can make you rich!*"

11 p.m.

Conrad pulled up to the tiny, dilapidated shack. The house stood alone on the empty dirt road, as if carved straight into the bleak, rural landscape. The only luminescence came from the moon and a flickering lamp inside the house. He crossed waist-length weeds and stepped onto the porch. Imagining he heard a raspy voice telling him to enter, he went inside.

The stench of rot and decay overwhelmed him. Newspapers and rusted junk were piled everywhere. The old woman – tiny, hunched over, smoking a cigar – came out of a bedroom, where Conrad could see flies buzzing about. She pointed to a chair by a table and they sat.

Conrad withdrew the chestnut box and placed it before her. She opened it and looked inside, her mouth agape. *There they were.* The five sisters set snugly in their place holdings.

"It's true then," she said.

Conrad nodded.

She withdrew a folded-up cloth and gingerly unraveled it. And then he knew. *This was the one.* For the first time, ever, he beheld the true *Sixth Sister*

"May I?" he asked with deep humility.

She handed it to him with the grace of a tragic soul finally acquainted with her heretofore unknown twin. Conrad cradled the knife, delicately. It seemed to pulsate with life.

"Go on," she prompted. "See if she fits."

He lowered it into the chestnut box – into the open compartment that had been waiting more than 100 years. The knife slipped in comfortably.

He reached into his jacket pocket and withdrew a checkbook.

"No," she said, closing the box and pressing it towards him. *"This is where they belong. Together."*

"But," he stammered.

"You have to go now," she said. "They'll be here soon."

"Who?"

"The police."

He had only driven a hundred feet when he heard the gunshot. He looked back, terrified, then quickly sped off.

12:30 a.m.

And Conrad was back in his hotel room, in his *perfect moment* with all six sisters laid out before him, the pursuit of his entire adult lifetime finally realized

Exhausted, he fell into a deep, fevered sleep and dreamt of viciously murdering family and friends and soaking in the blood of butchers.

When he awoke, he was sick and sweating, but knew what he had to do.

1 a.m.

The Elk's River bridge.

Conrad looked out over the cold, raging waters. He raised the chestnut box high above the handrailing.

"Don't do it!"

McCoy raced towards him.

"*It's no good!*" yelled Conrad.

"I'll get you whatever you want!"

"Don't you understand?! They won't be sold! They won't belong to anyone! *This has to end!*"

He dangled the box over the handrailing. McCoy pulled out his gun.

"Give me the box, Conrad."

Conrad threw it over. Without thinking, McCoy fired. Conrad collapsed, clutching his side. Then bright headlights were shining on both of them.

"*Stay where you are!*" called the police.

But Conrad was dead.

No one noticed the tramp under the bridge who had awoken to the sounds of the two men arguing, seen the chestnut box fall, and heard the gunshot fired. The tramp quickly waded into the water to retrieve the box, but was disappointed to discover only an old set of highly tarnished steak knives inside. Regardless, he dried them out and sold them to a nearby two-star bistro for $20 and a bowl of clumpy chowder. Soon after, the bistro manager discarded the box and simply mixed the cutlery in with his other tableware.

And so, it was on an unremarkable Tuesday evening when a family of four – father, mother, son, and daughter – came in for a hot meal. And as the father cut into his bloody filet with the *Sixth Sister*, he felt suddenly that he would enjoy nothing more than to ruthlessly slaughter his wife, son, and daughter.

Perhaps that very evening.

Groucho in the Bardo

The Bardo. A misty, foggy place. RUFUS T. FIREFLY, slightly hunched and with well-manicured greasepaint, wanders about lost. There are sounds of faint WAILING and CRYING.

FIREFLY: Hello! Hellooo! Either I'm in Hell or the world's worst sauna.

CHICOLINI, sporting his Tyrolean fedora, appears – also lost. They both creep about, not seeing one another. Chicolini raises his fists, ready to fight.

CHICOLINI: Who's-a dat? I hear you, but I no see you! And that's two-a you, I already don't like!

They slowly back into each other and collide, surprised. They're approximately pleased to see one another.

FIREFLY: I should've known it was you – fog follows you everywhere.

CHICOLINI: At's-a true. Hey! This is some barbecue! I think you left the steaks on too long.

The mists momentarily clear and a large signpost appears with the sign "THE BARDO" tacked onto it. They read the sign.

FIREFLY: Ah! We're in the Bardo!

CHICOLINI: Well, sure!

FIREFLY: I knew it all the time!

CHICOLINI: And why not?! (*beat*) What's a Bardo?

FIREFLY: Beats me.

Firefly eyes the sign. There is tiny print on it.

FIREFLY: Hey! Wait – a – minute. It says here (*reading*): "YOU – ARE – DEAD!" (*cheerily*) Well, now it's all clear.

CHICOLINI: Ah – that don't sound so good.

FIREFLY: I was feeling under the weather. And now I'm completely submerged. I tell you – I suspected we were dead!

CHICOLINI: Yeah, I thought so too. What gave it away?

FIREFLY: You did! Mostly the smell.

CHICOLINI: Oh, that's not me. (*withdrawing a sandwich*) That's–a just my sandwich. It's not so good anymore.

FIREFLY: How long have you had it?

CHICOLINI: What time is it?

FIREFLY (*checks his watch*): 10:30.

CHICOLINI: Three weeks. (*beat*) It's an emergency sandwich! Never know when you gonna need an emergency sandwich.

FIREFLY: Well, you won't need it now.

CHICOLINI: Why not?

FIREFLY: Because you're dead, you –!

A HONKING SOUND is heard. PINKY, wearing a top hat and massive overcoat, and grinning manically, enters through the mist.

CHICOLINI: Pinky!

Pinky and Chicolini embrace and dance around.

FIREFLY: Well, you never can have too many morons in Hell.

From one of his large pockets, Pinky pulls out a sandwich, and hands it to Chicolini.

CHICOLINI (*thrilled*): Liverwurst! Pinky – you crazy!

FIREFLY: Oh – *he* gets a sandwich? What do *I* get?

Pinky hands Firefly a large rubber fish.

FIREFLY (*to audience*): You should see the one that got away.

SOUNDS of WAILING grow louder. Pinky looks around the empty fog, pushes his tongue out, fearfully.

CHICOLINI: Pinky – it's okay! We're in my Bardo!

FIREFLY: *Your* Bardo?! It's *my* Bardo!

CHICOLINI (*preparing to fight*): It's not your Bardo! Since when is it your Bardo?!

FIREFLY: Since I claim it! (*proudly, an explorer*) I claim this Bardo – *for me!* See, now it's my Bardo.

CHICOLINI: Ah – y'got me. Fair and square.

MARGARET DUMONT, plump and matronly, wanders on, lost and nervous.

DUMONT: Hello?!

Firefly swoops in front of her, flirtatious.

FIREFLY: Well, *hello!*

DUMONT: It's so misty! I can't see anything!

FIREFLY (*averting his eyes from her*): I wish I couldn't see anything. I mean – Madam – you're ravishing!

DUMONT: Where are we?!

FIREFLY: Welcome to my boudoir! Excuse me, Bardo!

CHICOLINI: *His* Bardo! Pfft!

FIREFLY (*to Chicolini*): Don't you have a train to catch?

CHICOLINI: I caught too many trains today. I gotta give some back.

Pinky HONKS loudly, looks off into the mist. The others look also. The WAILING is LOUDER.

CHICOLINI: Ats-a Abe Lincoln! I useta play with his logs!

Pinky nods, produces an entire miniature log cabin from his coat.

CHICOLINI: Ah – that's pretty good! Hey – he looks sad! Maybe we bring him a sandwich?

Pinky nods, and he and Chicolini head off into the mist. Firefly turns his attention to Dumont.

FIREFLY: Alone at last! Well, except for you, here. (*beat*) Have I told you I love you?

DUMONT: Well –

FIREFLY: Don't interrupt!

Firefly gets down on one knee.

FIREFLY: My darling! Come get lost with me!
Better yet, you get lost by yourself.

DUMONT: Excuse me?!

FIREFLY: My dearest, I adore you! Marry me!
Marry me – and all this can be yours!

DUMONT: The Bardo?

FIREFLY: Yes. I just had the fog upholstered. Marry
me, and all you can see is yours!

DUMONT: But all I see...is nothing!

FIREFLY: Exactly.

The WAILING becomes terribly LOUD.

DUMONT: What is that awful noise?!

*ROLAND, extremely bland, comes on, singing I'm in
the Mood for Love poorly. The sound of WEEPING
and GROANING in response to him is DEAFENING.*

FIREFLY: Well, that's no surprise.

Roland, panicked, runs off. Firefly takes Dumont in his arms and dips her, romantically.

FIREFLY: Where were we? Oh yes – *I love you!*

Chicolini returns with a very young, French BRIGITTE BARDOT.

CHICOLINI: Hey! Look who I found! It's-a Brigitte Bardot!

Firefly drops Dumont to the ground.

FIREFLY: Well, *hello!*

BARDOT: Allo!

CHICOLINI: See! Now, we got Bardot in the Bardo! At's-a something, hey?!

Bardot looks around, nervously, shivering.

BARDOT: Why ees eet so foggy and steenky!

FIREFLY: It's probably his sandwich.

The HONKING is heard again. Pinky returns, dragging in GRETA GARBO in a pants suit. They all stare at her, amazed.

BARDOT: Greta Garbo! C'est magnifique!

Pinky HONKS delightfully.

CHICOLINI: Garbo in the Bardo! At's a good one, Pinky!

GARBO: Where in God's name are we?

FIREFLY: Just a little soiree I threw together.

GARBO: I hate soirees!

FIREFLY: Well, pardon my Bardo! (*to the audience*) You thought I was going to say, "sorry for the soiree." We changed that this morning. Never read from an outdated script.

DUMONT: Well, I've had just about enough!

BARDOT: And oooo are you?

DUMONT: I am Margaret –

BARDOT: Margeuax?

FIREFLY: Close enough.

CHICOLINI: Ho–kay! We make introductions!

Chicolini and Pinky run around the three women manically shaking their hands, bumping into them, climbing on them, and knocking them over. Eventually, Firefly, sensing a good thing, joins them. Pinky HONKS continuously.

CHICOLINI: Garbo Margeuax, Margeuax Bardot, Bardot Margeuax, Garbo Bardot Margeuax Margeuax, Garbo Bardot Bardot Margeuax, Garbo Margeuax Bardot Margeuax Bargo, Bardot Garbo Mango Mardo Bargo Bingo Bango Bongo!

DUMONT: I'm so confused!

Pinky hands her the rubber fish. She recoils horrified. He laughs wildly, silently.

DUMONT: Oh God!

BARDOT: I don't like zees place! I want to go home!

The SOUND of an LOUD ENGINE REVVING is HEARD. A MOTORCYCLE with a sidecar pulls up, driven by a young MARLON BRANDO in full–on biker gear.

FIREFLY: Brando!

CHICOLINI: In the Bardo!

BRANDO: Who needs a lift?

FIREFLY: Me!

BRANDO: Uh – who else?

BARDO: Oui oui!

Bardot climbs on the back of his bike. Dumont gets into the sidecar. The three ride off.

FIREFLY: There they go – Brando and Bardot.

CHICOLINI: Right outta the Bardo.

Pinky HONKS. They notice they're alone.

FIREFLY: Where's Garbo?

CHICOLINI: Ats–a good question. Maybe she wasn't really here?

Firefly looks around, distraught.

FIREFLY: Oh – despondence my old, old friend.

CHICOLINI: Is he really your old friend?

FIREFLY: Yes, but he owes me twenty bucks. (*beat, cheering up*) Say...I'm famished! Let's eat!

Pinky snaps his fingers, pulls a gigantic hero sandwich out of his coat and divides it between the three of them. They all slump down and eat.

Suddenly, LINCOLN enters, joyfully, eating his own sandwich. He smiles appreciatively at the boys.

LINCOLN: Liverwurst! Yum!

BLACKOUT

Somewhere Other than Earth

SPACE. A tiny, 1950's-era, Buster Crabbe-type rocket vaults through the cosmos.

BOOMING NARRATOR: Fleeing from an Earth overrun by bluster and pomp, Mark Savage and his pal, Dani, wander the stars in their two-person rocket, Charcuterie! Their destination: *Somewhere Other Than Earth!*

A DENSE JUNGLE. MARK and DANI – in space outfits – make their way through a clearing. Suddenly, they're ambushed by four ferocious monsters: GORGO, RODAN, MOTHRA and KONG.

RODAN: Humans!!!

MARK: We come in peace!

The monsters circle them, warily.

DANI: Is this the Planet of Unqualified Exchange Students?

MARK: Is it the Nicki Minaj Weight Loss Planet?

KONG: No! This is the Planet Where Everyone has Deja Vu!

DANI: But we just left a – hold on –

MARK: What?

DANI: I think we've done this, already –

MONSTERS: No! Not at all! This is a completely new planet!

DANI: No... see, I think *you* had an e-book, and *you* were, like, doing a yoga, tree-thing pretty badly. Right? C'mon.

GORGO: We are one hundred percent different monsters than you've ever seen before! ARGGG! ARAGGH!!

MOTHRA: Actually, I am vaguely unsettled by her suggestion.

KONG: Kill them! Even though this all seems oddly familiar!

Mark whips out his ray-gun.

MARK: Alright! That's enough! Get back! (*to Dani*) Okay, I totally remember saying that before.

DANI: See? Let's just leave.

The monsters stare at them, befuddled. Mark and Dani back away, cautiously.

MONSTERS: Well...that's probably okay. Have a lovely day. Don't drink and drive.

Mark and Dani exit, nonchalantly. The monsters stare at each other, somewhat frozen.

BOOMING NARRATOR: Where will Mark and Dani find themselves next?! *Somewhere – wait – did I say this already? Wow, I have a headache. What does "booming" mean, anyway? Is my voice booming? Or do I explode or something? I'm so confused.*

The Sleep of Angels

I'll be home for Christmas

It's cold. It's dark. It's 6:50 a.m. in red, hellish figures. I wake up every few minutes to the *pit pit pitting* of snow. Still snowing. And I don't move. If I move I get colder.

Katie's back asleep now. She's breathing, shivering, I think. She seems warm. She always gets very warm at night. Much warmer than I remember people getting. I've got an incredible headache. I guess – a concussion. If I'm lucky. The back of my head itches where the blood dried. I'm waiting for morning. For sunlight. Which should be in another – half hour? And then, hopefully, things will change.

I had a concussion in tenth grade when somebody clocked me from behind with a stapler on the last day of school. And I went down and there was blood all over and a scrape and a huge goose-egg. Just like this.

I think I ate too much candy.

11:30 p.m.

"Are you okay?! Are you okay?!"

"No. No!! I'm not okay. I'm not okay!"

"Okay, okay – oh my God. My car. Are you hurt?"

"I don't know."

"Your nose is – your nose is bleeding."

Katie looks in the passenger mirror. A drop of blood dangles at her nostril. Her eyes well up.

"Okay. Let's not panic. Let's try to relax."

"I'm not panicking!"

"I'm not saying you're panicking. I'm saying we could panic – but let's not."

"Don't tell me what to do. If I want to panic – *I'll panic.*"

"Fine – but we're both probably in shock right now. I'm *definitely* in shock."

"God. We have to get home!"

"We'll get home. We'll get home."

I take off my seatbelt.

"Where are you going?"

"To get it off my car."

I get out of the car onto sleek ice and survey the situation, which is a frozen shit storm. It's Christmas Eve. Snow's beating down hard. We're an hour-and-a-half from her parents' house stuck on a "shortcut" to the middle of nowhere. My car – a '03 Celica – rests half off the road in a snowbank. Windshield's cracked.

And there's a deer on my car.

A big one.

"Is it dead?!"

"It's very dead."

"Can you get it off the car?"

The deer appears to me to be a gigantic, grown male deer. A buck. It's probably a baby. But I'll tell people it's a grown male. Because the last thing I want to hear is how a baby wrecked my car. Its eyes are wide open. I pull at it, uselessly.

"Can you get it off?!"

"No."

Katie comes out, stares at the mess, pissed. I hit the deer. Could've been her. She could've been driving, easily. But it was me. I hit the deer.

"Help me pull its head!" I say. "Pull! Pull!"

"It's too heavy! God! Aren't we supposed to be getting some kind of adrenaline rush to help us, here?!"

"I've *got* one!!"

Katie gives up, quickly.

"I can't stay out here!" she says. I'm freezing!"

She pulls out her cell phone.

"Who are you calling?"

"Triple A." She pauses, stares at it. "I can't get a goddamned signal! Try your phone!"

"My battery's dead. Keep trying!"

"Stop yelling at me!"

"I'm not yelling at you. Stop yelling at *me!*"

Back inside the car. My head against the wheel. Katie stares off, her anger, a small, effective space heater. She notices the deflated canvas bag plopped around my steering wheel, and the absence of one on her side. Her eyes glower at me in the dark.

"My air bag didn't inflate."

"I know…"

"You said you were going to take it in!"

"I know."

"How could you not do that?!"

"I was going to – I meant to –"

"I could've been killed!"

"I know."

"Yours came out! Yours inflated!"

"I know. *I know!* I don't – I don't even know how to get it back in..."

The deer stares at me through the windshield.

"I asked you to take it in! To make an appointment. How could you not do that?! This is exactly *why* you were supposed to take it in!"

"I know."

"I could've been killed!!"

"*I'm sorry!* Next time –"

"*Next time!!?*"

Outside again, pulling. *Now*, I have an adrenaline rush. Now, I will pull the deer off my car.

"NNNNnnnnggg!"

Katie sticks her head out the window.

"Joe!"

"NNNNnnnnggg!"

"Joe! Don't be –"

"GET OFF MY CAR!" I yell at the deer. I *hate* the deer. The deer is my enemy. The deer is fucking up my life.

"Off my car! Get – off!"

"Don't take your anger out on the deer!"

"The deer is dead! Who cares whether I take my anger out on it or not?!"

"It's not right!"

"*It's staring at me through the goddamn windshield!!!*"

Katie comes out. Carefully, checking her revulsion, she reaches over and gingerly pulls the deer's eyelids down. I look around. Except for the car, no light appears from any direction, maybe for miles. I look at Katie. She looks at me.

"I think," I say, "we're fucked."

12:12 a.m.

Snow tumbles down harder. We determined that the Celica has no traction behind its rear tires. We determined this by shoving my overnight bag under the left rear tire, revving the engine and effectively burying my bag under several feet of ice and snow. There was never this much snow in New York. Where did it all come from?

"Okay," I say. "Okay. People should be coming by. Cars. There's got to be a lot of travel on Christmas."

At midnight? On this road that was a "secret" between her and her father? Yeah, no. But I don't say that.

"We've got heat. And light."

"Until the gas and battery go."

"If someone comes by – they'll see us. They'll stop. They'll call the police. Triple A. The sheriff. Tow trucks will come. Someone will come. If even one person comes – we're fine. Or –"

She says nothing.

"Or," I say, "we could go find a house. One of us – or both of us – could go find a house. A farm. Katie?"

She's having one of those internal meltdowns where nothing rational matters. Her "giving up" mechanism kicks in, instead of the "taking action no matter how useless" one I've got.

"Katie, we can't just sit here. I think – I bet we could find a house –"

Nothing.

"Okay –"

I open the door. She jerks her head over.

"Close the door."

"Katie –"

"Look at it."

I look out the window. Snow flurries the size of large autumn leaves pelt down heavier, heavier. I can't remember snow falling like this. It would be romantic if it weren't so –

"Katie – it could be snowing all night. It could get worse. If we're going to go – we should go now. I can go."

"You'll get lost."

"I won't get lost."

"There're no lights!"

"I'll stay where I can see the car's lights."

She stares out the windshield at nothing, breathes deeply.

"My father will come."

"Katie..."

"He knows we're coming. He knows this road. When we're not there by midnight, he'll get worried. By one o'clock he'll come looking. He'll bring the truck. He'll get the deer off. He'll tow us."

"We don't know that," I say. "What if he doesn't?"

She stares out the window, confident.

"He will."

1:16 a.m.

I'll be home for Christmas, you can count on me

Katie burrows next to me. We watch the flakes fall. Share an iced tea. We've eaten through one tin of Christmas cookies and we're working on the candy. Survival instincts.

We've played twenty questions sixteen times. We've named states, cities, fictional characters and rock bands, both alphabetically and starting with the last letter of each last word/name. She's told me about an uncle she never knew who recently died while swimming to lose weight. We've had conversations about smoking. About who we liked when we were kids. What we lost. Conversations about winning contests at radio stations. And about how, 21 years ago, I punched a kid at camp and maybe I shouldn't have, and this is punishment. We've had conversations about assertiveness training, the internet, farm life, libraries, exchanging places with someone who has the exact same name as you and how long it would take people to tell the difference. We've had conversations about why so many people wear black, breaking up with people by correspondence, great memories of doing nothing, weird hats, trying to follow the stock market and Houdini.

We've reached the caroling part of our evening.

Have a holly, jolly Christmas and a happy New Year

Oh by golly, have a holly, holly, jolly, holly, jolly...

"That must have been the most enjoyable Christmas song anyone ever wrote. *Holly, jolly, good golly Miss Molly...*"

Katie traces the crack in the windshield with her finger, smiles.

We three kings of Orient are...

"What?"

"*What?*"

"We three kings of Orient are *what?*"

"Kings of Orient."

"So, it's 'we three kings of Orient are kings of Orient?'"

Katie shrugs.

We three kings of Orient are...

...incontinent

We need Depends to circle the globe

Camelback riding's hard on the bladder

"Shh."

Katie perks up, startled.

"What's that?"

"What?"

"That sound."

"I don't hear anything."

"Wolves."

She grips me tighter.

"They're coming for the deer. They're going to eat the deer."

"Well...let them. It's their right. We'll stay in the car."

She shivers.

"My dad should've been here by now."

"He wouldn't've just – fallen asleep? We were coming pretty late."

"He waits up. And if he did fall asleep – by morning he'd come looking. If we're not there tomorrow, he'll come."

"Anyway, it'll be light in the morning. It'll stop snowing. It'll be easier to find a house, flag someone down..."

She looks at me.

"Joe. If I fall asleep – don't go anywhere."

"Go anywhere?"

"Don't get out of the car. Wander off."

"Where am I going to go?"

"To find help."

"I'm going to just leave you – without telling you – to go find help? Katie..."

"I'm serious!"

"I'm not going anywhere. And if I did, I'd *tell* you, first."

"Just don't do it. Promise me."

"I won't."

She shivers. And suddenly I hear wind. Trees. Maybe even animal sounds. But not wolves. I won't hear wolves.

2.02 a.m.

We've been quiet. Turned off the car for a while. Rationing gas. We've settled into the evening. I'm talking, but to myself. Things I've said a million times, just to hear myself talk.

"The perfect journey – driving. Perfect paradigm for a journey. Point A to point B. A map. A goal. A destination. It's a microcosm of – of everything. Of life. Aging. Except when you hit a deer and get stuck in a ditch. But then that's part of the journey. Doesn't change anything. You go with it."

Katie presses against the far door. When I reach out to her, she flinches – doesn't want to be touched.

"This is what happens," she says. "They find old ladies. Frozen in their cars by the side of the road. Weeks after they're dead. No one ever finds them.

Hundreds a year. *Hundreds.* I've read about it. They do what we're doing. Nothing. They sit and wait and freeze and die. Or that couple whose car broke down in the snow and they found a cave. Sure, they live, but they lose fingers, toes..."

"Katie..."

"I don't want to lose fingers or toes!"

"We're not —"

"I don't want to be tested by God! I just want to be bundled up on my father's sofa drinking cider! At least the couple in the cave had a baby. Something to protect. We don't even have a baby. We just have each-fucking-other..."

She looks at me. She has dark rings under her eyes. All the cookies are gone, the candy, beef jerky. She stares at me.

"Joe...did you ever cheat on me?"

Here we go.

"Did you ever cheat on me?"

"Katie."

"Honestly?"

"I never cheated on you."

"Did you ever kiss anyone else?"

"No."

"I did."

"Look —"

"I don't want to die knowing I kept anything from you. I want to be honest with you. About everything."

"We're not going to die, Katie. We don't have to —"

"I fooled around with Allan Womack. We didn't have sex."

"It doesn't matter."

"In Atlanta."

"I know."

"You didn't know."

"I assumed that if you were ever going to fool around with anyone it would be Allan Womack in Atlanta. Okay?"

"You're so smart. You know everything – you're such a genius."

"Katie –"

"Why didn't you charge your fucking cell phone?"

"You wanted to tell me! So, don't get pissy with me!"

"We fooled around after that, too. A couple times. We never had sex."

"I forgive you."

"I didn't like him. I hated him. But I was miserable. I'm sorry. I'm sorry."

"Whatever."

"And..."

"Oh god."

"...I had sex...with a guy...at the Brian Setzer Concert."

I look at her. She chews, manically, on the fingertips of her glove.

"I was *with* you at the concert."

"Not in the bathroom."

And then I suddenly feel like I'm with someone I've just met for the first time. And I appreciate the importance of secrets and lying.

"I didn't even want to *go* to that concert," I say.

"I know. You were being so rotten and negative that night..."

"I'd just gotten *fired!* How was I supposed to act?! Cheerful?!"

"I know. I'm sorry. Do you forgive me?"

"*No!*"

"No?"

"I don't forgive you! Why should I forgive you?!"

"You forgave me for Allan Womack."

"I'm not your stupid priest! I'm under no obligation to forgive you for anything!"

"I told you a secret! I didn't have to tell you!"

"You didn't have to fuck some guy in a bathroom *on my birthday!!*"

"And I wouldn't've if you weren't such an *asshole that night!*"

A wall of cold. Solid. Gaseous. I envy the deer. In deer heaven, frolicking. Let wolves eat him. What do I care?

"Peggy," I say. "Peggy Giordano."

"Now, you're just saying that to hurt me."

"Bowling night. When we were all out till one in the morning? There was no bowling. It got canceled. We stayed in the office and worked. For a while."

"Don't. Just don't."

"I'm clearing my conscious. Do you forgive me?"

"Fuck you."

"This is *your* game. Do you forgive me?"

She screams. She beats and kicks at my glove compartment, kicking dents, holes in the plastic. She kicks the windshield spreading the crack farther into thousands of tinier veins. I tear off my seatbelt, open the door.

"I'm going for help."

I step out onto slick, sloped iced. Falling, I gash my side on the open door. And then.
Nothing.

And I'm at home. Her parent's home. In bed. Katie's gone downstairs, but let me sleep. Sunlight comes in from the windows, but I'm so comfy, under huge down comforters. I appreciate blankets, cotton, warmth. So tired I never want to get up. I hear all the chit-chatting downstairs. I smell bacon, coffee. There's a deer at the front of the bed, grazing, keeping me from getting up. But I don't mind. Katie's father watches us, smiles. I'm content. I'm home.

And the deer is Jimi Hendrix, suddenly, dressed in dark glasses with a fringe Nehru jacket and huge afro. And the deer plays slowly, heavy jamming on his electric guitar...

Silent night
Holy night
All is calm
All is bright
Round yon virgin, mother and child
Holy infant, so tender and mild
Sleep in heavenly peace

Katie leans over me. Her face is puffed and red like someone who's been crying a long time. She touches my head, gently. My head – my head is pounding. I'm still in the car. I vaguely remember leaving the car and now, magically, I'm back. Something has happened.

"Joe...Joe...I'm sorry. I'm sorry."

"What happened?"

"You fell on the ice. You hit your head."

My head? I reach back. There's a shirt wrapped around my head. I touch wetness. Blood. Lots of blood on my hand.

"It's okay. You're okay. It's just...a little cut."

"Uh huh."

"I'm sorry, Joe. Don't leave the car again. We'll wait. We'll be okay. I love you."

"I love you, too."

She gently lays her head on my chest. I flinch as spasms of pain shoot through my head. She lifts up, quickly.

"*Sorry!*"

She puts her head back down, gentler, causing more spasms. I put my arm around her.

"My father will come. Someone will come..."

"Uh huh."

"It doesn't matter. We're with each other. That's all that matters."

"I didn't sleep with Peggy," I say. "We did go bowling. I never cheated on you."

"It doesn't matter."

"I can't see the clock."

"It's four-thirty. You were out for a long time. I thought you were –"

She's crying again.

"I'm not. I'm fine."

I hold her, noticing motor control of my fingers. I wriggle my toes. Flex my muscles. I take this as a good sign. Perhaps I've "passed" one of those tests. Katie soaks my shirt, crying. She's tired.

"We should've never gone home for Christmas. We're so stupid!"

"Let's sleep, Katie. Let's get some rest."

"I love you."

"I love you, too"

And she kisses me like she won't be kissing me again. Like she has to taste it. Like we're the first boy and girl in the first car at the first drive-in ever. My brain throbs and I kiss her, thinking I will pass out but that's okay. And then, gently, being careful to keep the "bandage" against my head, she pulls at my pants, pulling off my shoes, socks, tearing them off. Undressing herself, quickly, desperately.

As she presses against me I think about how we never bring contraception to her parents because - why? We sleep separately. At her parents, we're sexless for all intents and purposes. I think about it. And then I don't.

She climbs on, doing all the work. The bandage slips off and I think, well, it'll heal faster with exposure to air. As she moves naked in my arms, I imagine the lights of her father's truck pulling up, bright flashlights shining through the window. *This is what I drive an hour in the middle of the night for?! Say! That's some deer! You do that yourself?*

5:00 a.m.

Katie sleeps and I go in and out. Something bothers me, but I don't know what. Something about being buried, covered over – buried in a warm, steel grave of snow. I shouldn't care – but...if we're buried...if the car is covered, buried...but warm. Katie against me, coughs, sweats. The car chugs away.

"Katie..." I hear my voice. Rasping. My throat, raw. I jab at her. "I have to turn the car back off, Katie. The engine. I have to turn it off."

I turn off the car. She looks at me. Already, I feel chill's evil fingers creep over us. I can't even tell if it's snowing anymore.

"Why –"

"Exhaust. If car's covered, we can't keep engine on. Put your clothes on."

She pulls her clothes over herself, chattering. She pulls at my pants, closing them.

"I'll clear it in the morning."

She wraps herself over me, freezing. I drape my arms around her.

"We'll be okay. We'll be okay," I say. "I promise."

5:30 a.m.

When does the sun come up? Six? Six-thirty? What if it's up and we can't see it? How will we know it's morning and to leave the car? Is this what happens to them – those old ladies? They wait and fall asleep and never know when it's over?

Not me. All I have to do is get up. If it's daylight. Start looking for a house. Just get up. I'll wait till seven. Conserve my energy. The sun must be up by seven. I'll get up. I'll use the daylight. I can do it.

6:50 a.m. in red, hellish figures.

And I think of all the things I didn't say – didn't get to ask – like – *what was up with the acne? Why didn't you like to share your food? Why save things for last? What did you do with all that poetry? Why were you happier sleeping? Why didn't you tell them you had sex? That you liked it? Sometimes.*

And did I change? Did my personality change? Over the years. What happened to us? To that shirt – that signed Dave Sim t-shirt I used to have – with the stain you couldn't get out, but managed to wash out his signature? He should've written his name in grease.

Why do I think the way I do? Why do I care about material things? When were we supposed to change the oil? What if you never finish Ulysses?

Things. Things.

That hair wasn't important. That you should've traveled more together. Should've had a kid. That you should've appreciated her more.

And now maybe it's too late.

"Katie..."

Nothing. And my body doesn't respond to me. It won't sit up, reach to her. I can't even see her face from this position. I don't think of it as cold anymore. It's just there. With me. With my body. Numb.

"Katie –"

Nothing.

"*Katie!*"

I kick at her. Keep kicking, again and again. I feel her move. She blinks at me, squinting. Her voice, raspy too.

"My throat hurts..."

But still with us. Still here. She closes her eyes, goes limp on my chest.

"Katie...don't sleep. Don't go to sleep. Soon now. Soon..."

I'll be home for Christmas
if only
in my

6:59 a.m.

Mechanical sounds. A truck. Shovels scraping. Brilliant light etching its way through the windshield and behind it – yellow, red – flashing. Thick, glove-covered hands rapping on the door. Eyes looking in at me, seeing me. A hand flashing an "okay" sign. Katie gripping me, tighter.

"Did we make it?"

I nod. She puts her head down.

And for fifteen minutes, while deer and frozen doors are slowly pried apart, she sleeps the sleep of angels.

About the Cover

The front and back covers were designed by the author, incorporating elements that first appeared in the following periodicals:

Adventure, May 18, 1918, George M. Richards, artist
Adventure, April 18, 1919 and January 10, 1922, Charles Livingston Bull, artist
Adventure, March 30, 1922, E.D. Weldon, artist
Mammoth Adventure, artist unknown
Planet Stories, artist unknown
Top-Notch Magazine, April 1, 1927, artist unknown

For more information on these and other fine pulp magazines, please visit www.pulpmags.org and www.philsp.com.

About the Author

Alex Bernstein lives in New Jersey and is the author of *Plrknib* and *Miserable Holiday Stories*. His work has appeared at New Pop Lit, The Big Jewel, MonkeyBicycle, McSweeney's, Cincinnati Magazine, Corvus, BluePrintReview, Encyclopedia Vol. 3, Hobo Pancakes, Gi60, The Rumpus, The Legendary, Yankee Pot Roast, Swink, Litro, Back Hair Advocate, PopImage, and Prom on Mars, among others. Please visit him at www.promonmars.com.

Made in the USA
Middletown, DE
04 December 2019